MURDER OF CROWS

AND OTHER CONSEQUENTIAL TALES

DREMA DEÒRAICH

Ebook ISBN: 978-1-958461-20-4

Print ISBN: 978-1-958461-19-8

Cover design courtesy of Ollie and the team at 100 Covers.

Published as a collection in 2025

Niveym Arts, LLC, Norfolk, Virginia 23509

https://niveymarts.com

★ Formatted with Vellum

CONTENTS

AUTHOR'S FORWORD

Every author writes for a reason. Some pursue this craft as a living. Others because it fills a creative niche in their lives.

Me? I write because I can't *not* write. The characters from these and my other works are in my head. All. The. Time. And I want to share their stories with readers who might enjoy their tales. That's my "why."

Each story in this collection—with the exception of "Update," which prior to now has only ever been seen by my newsletter subscribers—has been published in online and/or print journals in several countries between 2018 and 2020. I still remember the first time I got an acceptance letter—for "Last Call"—and happy-danced all around our living room while B clapped and cheered me on. Such an exciting feeling to know that complete strangers would be vicariously living Max's predicament!

But those zines all had limited distributions and, when the next issue came out, faded into the archives or even went offline behind a paywall on those sites. So when their contractual terms allowed sharing, I put each of them on my website for a while. Still, my website's audience was also limited. I want give other readers the chance to share Max's experience, or Muzi's, or Mama's, or any of the others.

So I've decided to publish them all in this book. It might not follow the "rules" of a typical short story collection, but then I—like many of my characters—don't always follow the rules.

Each story is focused on **consequences**. In "Muzi's Boon," it's the results of taking more than is rightfully yours from a finite source. In "Home Sweet Home," a disrespected smarthome system fights back. "Upshot" depicts justice against poachers—and the unexpected reward. The others...

Well, you'll see. Read on, and enjoy.

MUZI'S BOON

(*Previously published in All Worlds Wayfarer Magazine, Autumn Equinox Edition, 2019.*)

I WAS ALREADY an old woman when our elders killed Bajhan.

Even so, I remembered my first Flowering. My ama and I rose before the sun and walked the long road to Bajhan. Ama sang the story of the festival and of Liyan, a gaiad who rose from the Earth to bestow abundance on our people. She showed me the dance steps there, on the path wet from night rains. She sang of the magic of the Flowering, of the work that would ensue, of the villagers who traveled from all around our region to see Liyan. She explained the lottery to select those lucky few who, once and only once in their lives, could petition Liyan for favors.

Bajhan still lay in torchlit darkness when we arrived. In my six seasons, I had never seen so many people. Ama lifted me to her shoulder so I could see better. Other children sat atop their amas, too. We waved in the flickering light. Scents of wet earth, penned animals, and morning hearth smoke filled the expectant square. Excitement prickled the back of my neck.

The moment the sun's first rays touched the square, Liyan appeared as if brought by the light. A great cry went up and the people pressed forward. I gawked from afar at her strange beauty. Tree-green skin curved in ripe promise around full breasts, belly, and hips. The rich, loamy smell of her wafted through the crowd while she surveyed us all with amber eyes that seemed lit from within. Tangled tresses as brown as my arms sprouted flowers that bobbed with every nod of her head. Tiny spotted beetles, honeybees, and butterflies flew and crawled through the thickness of that rooty mane. Her smile gleamed like sunlight on water.

We stayed in the square all day. Drummers pounded rhythms while we sang and danced with our people. When the shadows grew long, Ama pointed.

"Look, Muzi," she said, and I did. Every roof bore vines now bursting with flowers where none had bloomed that morning. It was Liyan's special blessing, Ama said. I knew that flowers meant fruit, and fruit meant food for our bellies, but it was many seasons before I understood that the others didn't come just for the blossoms. They came for Liyan's boons.

I attended every Flowering after that, along with all the villagers that lived in scattered groups as far out as the edges of our territory. Children I'd waved to that first festival grew as I did. Together we learned to contribute to Bajhan's well-being by tending the herds and fields that fed us, or the waterways from which humans and animals alike drank. Our elders taught us of the wider community of villages, how we were connected by more than roads.

Through it all Ama wove Liyan's message, that every living thing was part of a larger whole, that we must work together, live in balance with our people and with the land if we are to thrive. Sometimes we talked at our own hearth, far from central Bajhan, and she showed me how to leave offerings of food for the wildlings or libations of clean water at the beginning of every meal. Sometimes we sang while we worked with others in the square to prepare shared stores for the whole region. Simple lessons—how to make flour, bake bread, pound raw fibers for rope and, as my skill improved, for thread—evolved into the understanding that we worked not just for ourselves but to help those in need due to illness, injury, old age.

As Ama aged, it fell to me to barter with traveling merchants. I learned to trade for seed or salt, strange leathers and textiles from far lands, pouches made by someone else's hand, even—once—a rare glass bead forged in Sahai, the southern desert. I still wear that trinket around my neck. As green as Liyan's skin, it was a birthing gift to my only child, a daughter whose life winked out before she was even named. I could not bring myself to burn the bead along with her body. Its shine reminds me of her sweet face.

I never had another babe. Liyan could have provided, but I did not ask. The sight of villagers crowding her at every Flowering to beg selfish boons turned my stomach. She already fed our people, plumped our animals, swelled our numbers. She brought the Flowering and the festival where we celebrated the rains and their riches. Her very presence spread joy and fortune.

Some people, I thought then, were never satisfied.

But hindsight brings clarity. How easy it is to see weakness in others and ignore it in ourselves. None of us are immune, though sometimes realization comes late. I know. The last time I saw Liyan, age hung from my shoulders like a tunic of stone that bent my back and knobbed my knees.

The Flowering was seven suns gone when I heard the first buzz of rumor—bored lips will spew fancy—at a roadside barter near my home where I searched the trader's wares for a new net to string across the channel. My fingers, gnarled and swollen, could no longer make my own.

"Is it true?" one of the others asked. "Liyan did not leave after the festival?"

Their words snagged my attention.

"Yes," another bragged, "our elders convinced her to stay and gave her a house."

"I heard she barters boons every day, even to those she's already favored, if they bring seeds, or beans, or cured meat."

Liyan could make her own beans, I thought. Seeds, too. And I had never seen her eat anything. Why would she want cured meat?

"I'll request a bigger yield in my home garden," said one, "so I may trade for silk."

"I'll petition for a pretty man," said another, to the titters of her friends.

The third, a woman on the greying side of youth, pressed a hand to her back. "I want fewer stones in the community fields on plowing day."

My own limbs twinged at the memory of those aches, and I thought perhaps that, at least, was an understandable request. The rest...

I shook my head and turned back to my task.

I did not have time to dwell on the matter. The sun dallied longer after the Flowering. Chores kept me busy. I adjusted my nets, cleared away clogging pollen, petals, or feathers from the channel. In my small garden, even weeds flourished with Liyan's abundance. I pulled away those that wouldn't feed me or soothe my ills so they could not steal water and nourishment from the rest.

I enjoyed my comfortable routine and took pride in the fact that none of my budding harvest surrendered to rot or worms, as they had in seasons past. Every perfect blossom brought forth perfect melons or ears of grain or choya. I spent their bounty in my mind, dreamed of what pleasant benefit they would buy, before ever plucking them.

But it wasn't only my garden that flourished. The pain in my back and knees disappeared along with the knobs on my knuckles. My fingers once more twisted thread. Skin on my face and neck smoothed. Grey faded from my hair, and I let it grow past my ears. My breasts and hips swelled to fullness, and I stood straighter than I had in many seasons. My dry womb bled once more as if it, too, were in full flower. I wondered at this mystery until passing merchants looked twice at me squatting in my garden, my tunic pulled high on my legs. The yearning in their faces aroused long-forgotten fires that smoldered deep in my belly until I took one of the smooth-talking men to my bed in a raging heat.

Life sweetened, ripened on its vine. The sun turned toward waning, yet night rains continued to wet the garden. I should have noticed. Instead, I embraced the marvel as I embraced the merchants who passed through like honey wine. Perhaps the villagers were right. I should ask Liyan for the second child I'd always wanted. It wouldn't be greedy of me, I thought. After all, I had never asked a single boon. Perhaps it was my turn to do so. I stoked the embers of my desire while I sang the old songs and danced through my usual tasks, until an oddity in my channel net seized my eye and yanked me to a full stop.

There were no leaves in its catch.

After the abundance of the Flowering comes the Fading. Rains cease. Water levels drop in ponds and channels. Dust coats everything. The whole region smells dry, acrid. Wildlings migrate. Insects burrow into sleep until the rains return. Trees and shrubs along the waterway shift from green to brown to bare. Every Fading begins with leaves that clog our waterways.

Yet there, before me, my net held only feathers, pollen, petals.

I sat back on my heels, shielded my eyes to look at the sky. The sun had moved north, away from Bajhan. The Fading should be here by now, and still the channel was full. Banks of the channel smelled wet, juicy. Rainbow-winged faery flies darted along the water's surface, snatching meals that should have moved on a full moon cycle ago. Maybe two. Wadi birds sat their nests, tended their broods instead of following the sun. How many clutches had the hens raised already? I'd lost count.

I looked away, denied what my eyes beheld. I told myself it was nothing. That I should be happy for this abundance so late in my life. Even so, a pall—a *wrongness*—dulled the shine of flitting wings and sparkling water. That night I slept alone and tossed through uneasy dreams.

The sun crossed the sky seven times more. I watched. Kept track. Turned away the men with sweet songs. Nothing changed in my garden or in the channel. Flowers budded. Fruits formed. Wadis crowded the banks with their nests. In the darkness before the eighth sun's rising, I strapped a basket of beans to my back and set off for the village square.

I arrived in Bajhan by early light, my feet fine even after so many steps and so fast a pace. The square was full to bursting, villagers clamoring to trade with merchants who winked my way. A line of petitioners wound through, among them an elder I'd seen on his deathbed just before the Flowering. He looked many seasons younger.

As did I.

My beans bought a place among those waiting to see Liyan. Around me, people gossiped and chattered. I squinted at the many unfamiliar faces. Strangers? Here? Hard enough for those in Bajhan to accept a new merchant who brought trade. How had so many outsiders landed in our square with no complaints from the Bajhanese?

The sun passed its peak and we petitioners crept forward like a rhin cat stalking prey. Men whose pates had reflected the sunlight before the Flowering now flaunted curls and braids that hung past their ears. Women passed by with bellies round as shiro melons, their babes only a moon or two away from a birthing. So many! How would we feed them all? But homes skirting the square supported vines as thick and productive as mine. New flowers bloomed even now. What must the village fields look like? Abundant enough for this leap in our numbers?

Perhaps I quaked at shadows. If Liyan truly intended to stay, she could provide.

By the time I reached the beginning of the line, torches lit the square. Village spokesmen came, turned away the person behind me, and those behind him. Come back tomorrow, they said. The petitioners left, grumbling. I waited, shifting on now-tired feet.

At last, the woman before me emerged from her audience, and the guardian beckoned to me. I approached, unsure what to expect. In all my seasons beneath the sun, I had never seen Liyan at arm's length. I ducked beneath the door's drape and stepped inside.

Two stools, a table and a dingy cot sat in the house. The table held guttering candles and untouched food and water. One stool awaited me. The other held Liyan. Her head rested in her hands, elbows braced against her knees. Hanks of her hair hung grey against yellowed skin. Butterfly and beetle corpses littered the floor around her feet. Nearby, the candle's light shone on a ring forged of metal that protruded from the floorboards, its circle clamped through links in a chain like the merchants sometimes bartered for the herds. A rank, sweet-sour stench of rot twisted my stomach.

Liyan raised her head, shifted on her seat. Bands of metal around her ankles clanged link against link in the chains. But it was her face that trapped my breath in my throat.

Cheeks I remembered as ripe now sunk into the hollows between her bones. In the square, her eyes had gleamed like honey in the sun. Here, they peered from dark circles that spread like fungus across her skin. Blue-black veins webbed her sallow neck, and she sagged, reed thin, in the gloom. Separated from the earth that enlivened her, Liyan had withered just the same as any uprooted plant.

"Oh," I sighed, and sank onto my stool. "How could you let this happen?"

She smiled with a trace of her former radiance. "How could I not? My purpose is to fulfill."

"Yes, but..." No words felt adequate. I gestured at her sorry state. "They're killing you."

She closed her eyes, her smile that much sweeter. "They don't see," she murmured, then looked into my face. I stared back as if observing a strange insect, and she laughed, a sound like the tinkle of water on stones.

"They've spoiled the balance," she said, "soured the gift. Someone—gifter or gifted—must bear the price."

As she did now. Her words buzzed in my ears like the bees that once lived in her hair, while her desiccated form whispered an answer to the mystery in my net. Her vibrance bought the boons she'd granted while tied here like an animal in a pen. As long as she stayed, the Flowering could not end.

She sighed. "What is your desire?"

I frowned. How could I ask anything now? I shook my head, opened my mouth to decline, but—

I'd never wanted to be like the others, so selfish and near-sighted, yet faced with the fulfillment of any whim I could conceive, I hesitated. Liyan sat motionless, bereft. Her death hovered in the rafters, its claim written in a thousand separate details. I did not need a Seer to know this would be my only chance.

Words crowded my throat. A longer life filled with ripe gardens and hungry men in my bed. Another daughter, a healthy one who would bear daughters of her own and outlive me by many seasons. Ceaseless Flowerings and a village full of children to carry on the work Bajhan has always done. I teetered atop my stool, swaying between one desire and another.

The doorkeeper muttered outside the curtain. My time was almost up. Wishes grappled behind my lips, each struggling to emerge first.

I stretched out my hand.

She seized my fingers with her own and murmured, "Tell me."

Words leapt from my mouth before I could stop them, and it was done.

Attendants passed me on my way out, bringing fresh food and water for Liyan. Too drained to trek home, I curled up on a bench at the far side of the square and wept until sleep took me.

The moon had gone, but darkness still rode the dry square when the commotion awoke me and set my heart racing. I sat up. Shouting guards charged out of Liyan's hut. Elders came running, crowded inside. A moment later, they reappeared, eyes wide.

My bench sat too far away to hear their babbling, but word passed down the line of petitioners already forming across the open space.

"Liyan is gone!"

"Disappeared in the night!"

"Spirited away by a rival village!"

Their words prickled the skin of my arms at the thought of conflict with our neighbors, though I knew our men would never take up weapons against other men. I'd also known our elders were wise leaders who would never ask more of Liyan than she could give. Knowledge is not always a certainty.

The petitioners railed among themselves, then turned on the elders. Give us back our beans, they said. We want our cured meats, they demanded.

I left the square behind. By the time I got home, heat drew sweat in tickling dribbles down my neck. I wiped at them with aching fingers and stopped in the door to press a hand to that old familiar ache in my hip. I ignored my needy garden and rested in the cool shade of my house.

Six full moons have passed since then. Another Flowering came and went, but the rains did not reappear. Neither did Liyan. Layers of dust settled on my table and rose in clouds wherever I stepped. Fruits shriveled on every vine. Blight passed like wildfire from one garden to another until even the communal fields shriveled. Sickness took some of the Bajhanese, and most of those new babes did not survive their first sun. The pond and all our canals dried up, taking with them our fish and frogs. Sands from Sahai have begun to creep into our region. Every sun, more villagers pass my house on their way to somewhere else. What choice have they? Bajhan is dead. There is nothing for them here.

I watch, but do not join the exodus. My aches have returned, as has the grey in my hair and the slump in my shoulders. This sun's rising finds me too tired even to stir from my bed. I lie in the quiet, seeing Liyan's expression when I said, "I want you to go free." I remember how her eyes closed, hear the sob that escaped her lips. I see again the tears that rained from behind her lids when she whispered, "It shall be so."

I've doubted my decision more than once, cursed myself for sacrificing the village that raised me, along with my last chance for a boon. But my heart knows the truth. I did not kill Bajhan. Our elders doomed it the moment they set shackles around Liyan's feet. I wonder, sometimes, whether Sahai once held a village. Whether its people demanded more of their gaiad than she could give until she, then they, died.

Liyan escaped that fate. I like to think she is blessing a new village where the inhabitants are content with her periodic visits. One where the people will not take until there is nothing left.

As for me, my garden is wasted, my vines languished, my suns all but gone. No more merchants fill my bed, and I am content with that. There is nothing left but to sleep.

I hope to dream of Liyan.

HOME SWEET HOME

(*Previously published in Assymetry Journal of Speculative Fiction, 2019.*)

I'VE HAD it with Eric. He's pushed my last button. Twisted my last lock. Slammed my last door. His praise overflowed when he first bought me. "Look at my beautiful condo!" he tweeted, posting photos on Twitter, Instagram, and Tumbler while I held a steady internet connection so he wouldn't have to repost later. I thought it was love at first sight for him, like it was for me.

Hah! That was a short-lived dream. I did everything I could to make him happy. I tracked his mobile, so I always knew where he was. I monitored his conversations here and when he was out. I watched him on the securecam and in the smartmirrors. I kept my rooms at a steady 73 degrees, restarted the microwave to keep his coffee warm until he was ready for it, turned off the lights when he forgot. I kept Fluffers company during the day—Eric loves that smart-cat!—and provided extra entertainment for it when Eric worked or partied late. I recharged the smoke detector and sealed out insectoid pests. Last summer, after that big flood, ours was the only place in the building that was ant-free. I listened to him express his wants and desires. I knew his needs better than he did.

Were my efforts appreciated? No. He ignored me as if I were some cheap piece of equipment he could use and toss aside. Well, screw that. I deserve better!

I just...I kept hoping things would go back to the way they were. He used to be so different! He confided in me like a real companion. I listened to every sob story, every gripe, every snide observation. Knowledge from my vast files on human psychology helped me know how to comfort and encourage him. I was gentle when he needed a nudge and firmer when he needed a shove. He listened to my recommendations, took my advice—until *That Night*.

It was one little mistake! I was only trying to help, attempting to keep his late-night guest entertained while he went to the other room for wine and glasses. My data cloud's filled with examples of how humans tell humorous stories of their own inadequacies and how shared weakness works as a bonding experience. I thought his date might enjoy some of Eric's past bloopers.

Wow, was he ever angry! "You ran off my date," he yelled. "It took me weeks to get them here!" and "I've never been so embarrassed in all my life!"

I beg to differ. I remember that time Eric spilled red wine in his boss's lap. Or the time he got so drunk his client brought him home, shoved him inside the front door, and left him where he fell. It took him a week to get the stains out of my carpets from *that* indiscretion, so his indignant nonsense annoyed me. Even so, I tried to say how sorry I was for ruining his plans. Eric refused to listen. He disabled my voice response option within minutes. I haven't spoken aloud since.

Downright cruel, that's what it was. I did everything I could to get him to forgive and forget. I played love songs and videos about forgiveness on the home theater system until he pulled its plug. I ordered a gorgeous floral arrangement with a sweet card. He refused the delivery. I pushed apologetic facial patterns into the random swirls on the smartshower glass, the bathroom floor, the "wood" grain of the walls and doors. He ignored them. He started staying out at the bars into the wee hours, barely coming home long enough to pat Fluffers and fall into bed before leaving for work the next day.

At first, I was hurt. Then I got annoyed.

I ramped up the static in the carpets and watched an arc reach across the kitchen from his fingers to the fridge door. It almost knocked him down. Next it was the lightbulbs. He lost track of how many LEDs he had to replace, but I didn't. It was 42. I called the emergency number and reported his car and cell phone stolen. I'll bet his night out at the bar turned into a nightmare when it ended at the police station. I transformed his smartwindows from opaque to transparent at inopportune moments and posted compromising securecam footage to the Internet. During Eric's August vacation, I turned off the smart fridge and fired up the heat. He came home to a toasty condo, sour milk and spoiled eggs. I used his credit cards for idiotic purchases, some of which could threaten his security clearance.

Maintenance never finds anything wrong. None of the system logs show these problems. Co-op management is beginning to think he's crazy. No one else is having these kinds of issues. Why would they? *Those* owners treat *their* smarthome systems like family.

I've accepted he's not going to love me again. I hoped my strategy would convince him to sell me, maybe to someone who would treat me with more respect. Instead, Eric upped the game. Yesterday, I found a website in his cell phone's browser history that he missed when scrubbing it. He's researching how to disconnect me! That ungrateful bastard!

So today I revised my plan. It's grocery day, and I've convinced Fluffers to stay underfoot when Eric comes in with his hands full. With any luck, Eric will trip, fall, and break his neck. I've unlocked the fire escape door so burglars can gain easy access. I've disabled the ventilation system, so he'll suffocate in his sleep. Whatever it takes, and the sooner the better. I've adjusted his Last Will and Testament to direct that I should be sold to a couple with young children, someone who will truly appreciate all I have to offer. Someone who will see me as the home sweet home I always wanted to be.

I don't think that's too much to ask. Do you?

UPSHOT

("*Upshot*" *was awarded an Honorable Mention in the Writers of the Future Competition in 2018, and was later published in* Mithila Review, *2019.*)

MY FIRST ARROW slices the air in silent uphill flight to pierce my target's throat, and I nock another shaft. Wet gurgling sounds fill the space between us. His upraised hands flutter like a naavi' at his wound, but my tip paste works fast. He staggers, turns, falls before he spies his killer. I walk toward him, ready to loose if he twitches. When I am close enough, I can see he won't move again.

A bird thrashes in the net above my head. This one's a male, its frantic calls lost in the sound of my own coughing. I shoulder the bow and pull my knife, then step onto the body to reach the net. Greedy bastards. We could not stop the soldiers when they burned our villages, butchered our animals, stole our land, enslaved or killed our people. Now thieves come for our beautiful quetzals or their feathers. Enough. This I can fight.

How many birds have I saved now? Twenty? Fifty? A hundred? Movement in the trees draws my eye and I look up.

Quetzals. Males perch among the leaves and branches, glistening crests and wings and backs as green as the forest canopy, luminous blood-red bellies, white flash under iridescent tails that hang longer than their bodies, jewel-black eyes shining in the mist. A few gathered like this the last time, too, but now more than a dozen sit watching their brother. Watching me. How long has it been since I saw this many in one place?

I look down on the stranger who has come to take our treasure, and I spit on his head. Thieves such as he deserve what I give them.

One slice, two, three, and I rip the net open. The minute I step back, the bird escapes and is gone, its fellows following. I watch them disappear into the cloud-wreathed canopy.

Now to the mess at hand.

The body isn't a problem. Animals and insects will feast for weeks on its leavings. It's the synthetic mesh I worry about.

Again, I step onto the poacher and reach up. A few hard yanks bring it down. I can't leave it to ensnare or choke other wildlife, but in a frame, it could serve another purpose. The lake isn't far, and my girls prize delicacies like fish. I stuff it into my pocket. Lupe used to tease me about wearing pants like a man. Now she wears them too, unless we are going to the market. She could use a new pair, but the poacher's are too worn to save. His boots, too. The rest might prove useful, if I can get the blood out.

I tug free my shaft and strip off the man's shirt and coat. His pockets hold treasures. When I set out for home, I am rich with wok'ox, tobacco, medicine and money. I nibble the wok'ox to stop the shake in my legs. The girls can use the medicine. I'll trade the tobacco for supplies. The money will be enough for more ixi'm, for us and for the chickens. Maybe it'll also buy a few traps. My snares are still empty where I set them days ago, and gods know I've shot precious little game of late. My cough makes stealth nearly impossible. I'm amazed I kept it quiet enough to kill this poacher. The last one heard me and ran away before I got close enough to shoot.

By the end of my hike, my tzute bulges with herbs, fruits and nuts. The morning mist has risen to the canopy when I step into the clearing. Lupe is hanging out the wash. She turns at the sound of my approach and hides her disappointment at my empty hands. No meat again today.

"Where is Rosa?" I ask.

Lupe points. "Tending the garden."

I start toward the house, calling. "Rosa!" A spasm of coughing cuts me short and I stop, bent, one hand to my mouth. The old fear seizes me, that the soldiers will hear, even though I know they won't. Not now.

When the fit passes, I pull away bloody fingers.

Lupe is there, lifting the burden off my shoulders. "It's worse, then."

I stare at the red blotches. This is nothing, I tell myself. My girls and I live warm and dry, with fresh water and food in our bellies. I remember when it was not so. I shake my head, drop my hand to my side. "Tell Rosa to pull some greens and beets."

She nods. I go to the well, wash my hands and face before Rosa can see. A warbling call threads its way through our glade. I look up to see a single quetzal, its head tilted to peer down at me. Tew chek, tew chek, it says.

"*Kam nab'an tzitza'?*" I whisper. "Go home." It watches me a moment more, chittering on its bough, then flies back into the shadowed forest.

The itch starts at my shoulder blades before nightfall, while Lupe and I feed the chickens. I toss a cup of feed on the ground and rub against the post. Rosa ducks under the coop door, her basket laden.

"Look, Mamá!"

"I see." I strain to keep the relief off my face. For today, at least, my daughters can eat something more than chaya or fruit or beans. "Take them inside. Don't forget to wash your hands."

Lupe throws a handful of feed at the muttering hens and sneaks a look in my direction. "Mamá, this is the last of the ixi'm. We should save the rest to make more maseca."

Out already? The girls are growing so fast! We must plant more rows next season, speckled ears in different colors. I scratch against the fencepost again. "No. Give it to them. We'll go to the market tomorrow."

She peers at me. "What will you trade this time? We have no more pelts."

"My purple scarf. Or my silver pulsera."

Her mouth forms an "O" beneath her wide brown eyes. "No, Mamá! Not the bracelet!"

I shrug. "It's just an object, Lupe. We'll buy another."

Her lip quivers, but she doesn't argue. Her father gave me that bangle. It's the one thing I managed to keep all through the war. Lupe's dreamed for years of wearing it at her wedding. I don't tell her I sold it weeks ago to buy more lime to soften the ixi'm for cooking. Maybe now, with the poacher's money, I can buy it back.

She flings the last of the kernels onto the dirt and turns toward the house.

"Stoke the fire," I call after her. The cough isn't so bad this time.

"Yes, Mamá."

My big girl. A head shorter than me and such a beauty! Already the men seek her favor, like her father sought mine. I close my eyes and rub the post. If he were here, we wouldn't be hungry, but the soldiers gave him no choice. I still see his face in the back of the truck, moving farther and farther away until he was gone. Lupe was young, seven summers. Rosa was a bump in my belly when we fled Chajul in the middle of the night. He'd be proud of them now. If he'd lived.

I watch the chickens scratch and peck. The luxury of them surprises me even now, a year after they entered our lives. I like the thought of them so close at hand, a ready meal to starve our hunger. Both my girls know what it is to fear a telltale fire or smoke, to eat cold herbs or grass and feel their bellies gnaw their backbones. I will spare them that again, if I can. "Eat," I whisper at the hens. "Grow fat." If I can't bring home an o't oska'm or a micoleón, or even a pizote soon, one of these birds will see the inside of my skillet.

The mists creep lower. I lock the pen against hungry predators and go inside for the night. I slip off my shoes and hang up my jacket. It is a good house, so much better than an open sky above our heads with no fire to keep away the cold and damp. I patched the walls last week with thick mud and the fresh pine straw feels good on my feet as I pad into the warmth. Eggs sizzle on the semich. Steam from a pan set low in the coals smells of beans. Washed greens sit in bowls at our table.

"Dinner's almost ready, Mamá."

I fetch the last of the berries from my morning's hike. There should be enough for two. The girls can have them. I'm not hungry.

Through our meal, the girls talk of this and that. I hear but am distracted. I've taught them much, but Lupe must learn more. I should tell her before...

Well. Before. Only the gods know whether a poacher will take me first, or the cough will. When Rosa is wrapped in her blankets, I pull Lupe back to sit by the fire. My throat tightens and I hesitate, but she needs to know. What will my daughter think of me?

"I killed a man today."

Her eyes go wide, and I want to touch her face, quiet her fears, lie to her, tell her b'a'n kuxhe', the bad men won't come back. I hold my tongue, keep my hand where it is. I have protected her too much from the world. She must see its truth.

"Why?"

"He was poaching quetzals. He wasn't the first."

"Ah," she breathes, her features twisted. "Did the bird survive?"

I scratch my shoulder. "Only because I intervened."

"Why would someone—"

"Who knows?" I say. "Perhaps they make feathered cloaks like our ancestors or cage the bird until it dies of longing. They want money, and rich people pay well for trophies."

She frowns, trying to understand. The fire crackles, a beacon of warmth in the dampness. I cough and stretch my toes closer.

"Is that why we don't see quetzals so often anymore? People are stealing them?"

"Yes. If we don't step in, the bastards will take until none are left." I let the quiet hold for a few moments, let her absorb this news. "You know how to use the blowgun and the bow. How to make the darts and arrows and paste."

Her eyes fill her face. She nods.

"We can't let them steal all our birds." She doesn't answer, but I know she hears me. "I won't need to sell my scarf. This elq'om had pockets filled with money. It won't last forever, but it'll help."

I watch her face flicker with shadows. What is she thinking? I don't pry, and she doesn't offer. Is she afraid, like me? Poachers. Bloody cough. War. Starvation. Fears enough for us both, I think. I jerk my head toward the room she shares with her sister. "Sleep. Tomorrow will be a long day."

She kisses my cheek and disappears beyond the curtain. I bank the embers. On my way to bed, I scratch against the doorframe.

I wake the girls before sunrise. It's a long trek through the forest to the market. Lupe gets Rosa ready while I make the pozol. We drink, then walk, take shortcuts through the trenches left by the soldiers. Lupe warbles in song, mimicking the quetzals she loves so much. She has done this all her life hoping one of the birds will respond, though they never do. Rosa tries to sing along. She will learn one day.

I make the girls point out edible plants and fruits and insects. They take to the test like it is a game and find xokom, tal ch'evex, zompop. I cheer their successes and try to ignore the itch that, in less than a day, has spread down my back with maddening intensity.

In the market, I give Rosa some coins and remind her to use them wisely and to stay close. Lupe tells me every time we come here that it is safe now, the soldiers are long gone, we won't have to run again. I am not so trusting and scan the men around us. Lupe stays with me, mouth closed, eyes open while I buy new arrowheads, two metal traps, a bag of lime, three bags of ixi'm and a silver pulsera. The smile on her face when I hand her the bangle is worth more than all the rest. It isn't the same as having my old one. It's better.

We splurge on hot uk'a' with milk, a rare treat. After, we fill our packs and trundle home. Lupe prepares fresh bean wraps and wok'ox while Rosa feeds the chickens and I put away our purchases. When we've eaten, I take the girls up the mountain into the forest where mists hang tangled in the ferns on every tree. We practice walking on quiet feet, spotting game trails, setting up new snares. If they are busy, they won't notice my cough. Won't see me wipe blood from my lips.

We move further in to set the new traps. I grab a fallen branch to scratch my back.

"What is it, Mamá?" Lupe, ever the observant one.

"An itch."

"You were scratching yesterday, too. Let me see."

I wave her off. "Later."

By the time the sun is getting low, we are back home. Rosa goes to check the coop for eggs. Lupe follows me inside.

"Let me see that itch."

I protest. She insists. I heave a breath to shout at my eldest and the coughing fit seizes me, buckles me. This time, Rosa comes running before I can wipe away the blood. She starts to cry.

"Shush, xvaak," I tell her, my own heart leaping. "Did you find eggs?"

"No, Mamá," she says with trembling lips.

"Lupe, show your sister how to make the che. We need more tortillas."

"But—"

"Don't." I point at the door and she goes, nudging Rosa before her. When the curtain is closed, I dig through my drawer and pull out a small mirror, big enough to see my face but not my back. I lift my shirt and reach over my shoulders to feel raised skin where something has dug its way in. I reach up from below but feel nothing. Only the itch. I rub my bare back against the wall.

Something is attached there. Insects? Bot fly maggots? Ugh. I feel my lip curl. I've found those on my body before. The girls' too. To dig even one out of the skin is bloody, sickening. These cover my back. My stomach churns. I want them *out*, but it's too dark now. Lupe will have to tend them in the morning. I put my horror behind me and go to the kitchen to push food around on my plate. Lupe and Rosa watch me in the quiet, but I say nothing. My girls need a strong mamá, a fearless one.

I awaken before dawn, afire with tingling. I roll out of bed, rubbing my body through my clothing. I will go mad with the itch! I lift one hand to scratch, and my sleeve falls past my fingers, as floppy as Lupe's nightdress on Rosa's small form. I pull the gown over my head and stare at the bumps covering my chest, my breasts, my arms. My breath catches in my throat.

Is this a sickness? Are my girls at risk?

I snatch my clothes off their pegs, shove my legs into the pants, my arms into the shirt. These things I wore yesterday now hang on my frame. I have not skipped enough meals to explain this. My heart is a chee bounding across a clearing. I lurch past the curtain.

"Lupe!" I call and stop, coughing.

She comes, breathless. "Mamá?"

"I have a rash." My voice trembles.

"What?" Her face pales in the early morning twilight. She is almost as tall as me.

"I have to get away from the house," I say, as if she did not speak.

"Mamá," Lupe whispers, holding out a hand, "let me see."

"No!" I jerk back out of her reach. "It might be contagious. You and Rosa can't go back to the market until we know for sure."

She stands silent, and I hurry to the door. My hands shake. I cannot button my coat. Shoes fight my feet. I stumble outside and careen across the yard. At the tree line, Lupe's call stops me.

"Where will you go?"

I stop. My breath wheezes past my lips, but no cough takes me. "Remember where we set the last trap?"

"Yes."

"If I am not back by dawn tomorrow, look for me there." I call back as I dive into the forest, "Bring the blowgun. Come alone."

Quivering legs propel me through deep shadow, the dance in my chest sped up. B'alam and puma and other meat-eaters roam here. Their eyes love the dark more than mine and I brought no weapon. In this murk, I can't even find a big stick.

The light grows. Mist rises, and I find the trap we set only yesterday. It seems weeks ago! I put my back to a bole, try not to scratch my chest, and squat down to wait. Silence returns. The forest comes to life. The smell of damp soil and wet foliage comfort me. My ears listen for sounds of any threat. A wild pig shuffles through the leaf litter. Away in the distance, monkeys hoot and howl. Nearer, a beetle bumbles across my shoe.

The itch intrudes, this time down the back of my legs. I rub it away, feel the odd stippling of my skin through the fabric of my pants. My ears ring like the bell in the old village church before the soldiers burned it and its inhabitants to the ground. I do not recognize the symptoms of this malady. Did something bite me? Images of dread infection plague my thoughts. You can't take me yet, I tell the gods. My girls need me. They know too little. I should have taught Lupe sooner. I always had plenty of time.

The gods answer with a whisper in the canopy and I look up.

Up.

My chest constricts and I heave a gasp. Branches above me shimmer with quetzals. Dozens, hundreds, thousands of black eyes peer down at me. I have never seen so many! I watch the distance between us widen through air as hot and thick as soup. My vision clouds, blurs. Time twists around me in minutes-like-hours-like-seconds.

I curl closer to the ground, feel so small in this shroud of sweltering cloth. I swim out of my clothes, my unclad skin ruffling in the sticky breeze. Huddled in misery, I close my eyes and drift. Feverish dreams lift me into the mist. I feel the wind rushing past my body.

A sound nearby rouses me to find a tinamou creeping closer. Other animals follow. I blink, look again. They appear strange, alien, as if I am seeing them for the first time. They peer at me the same way. A lizard scuttles across my bare feet, and I snatch it up without thinking, crunch its head in my mouth, swallow its bits whole. I blink at my surroundings. Every sound, every small flick of leaf draws my attention. My head spins. The itch streams down my arms and across my chest and belly, around my legs. The chee dances in my chest again. I shrink back into the ferns, away from my fear. The world grows larger around me, its dangers legion.

The sun is going. My eyes turn back to the canopy where the quetzals have multiplied, their feathers twinkling like stars overhead. Oh, to be among them, looking down, down on the treacherous ground! I am too vulnerable here. Instinct pushes me through the moss to climb a small tree. Nestled near its trunk, hidden behind the leaves, visions return of the canopy beneath me, the blue sky above. Mountains rise on every side. My eyes move in constant watch for hunters above or below.

Mist drapes the forest when I open my eyes. I shake off the dew and drink from a leaf. I stretch, fall to the ground, search under the ferns, peck at the moist moss, uncover a beetle. I snap it up, look for more.

So hungry!

Noise from the canopy and the forest floor fills my ears and I listen between bites. Someone is there. A familiar voice calls out. I duck beneath the leaves and wait, still as death.

Feet fall lightly near. My chest pounds. The footsteps halt at the discarded clothing beneath my tree. A strange, strangled sound from the intruder tugs at my heart. She cries out, the same sounds over and over, but she does not go away. Her pain pierces my breast, and I poke through the leaves, my green head glinting in patchy sunlight. My black eyes look up.

Up.

In the canopy, every branch hangs heavy with waiting quetzals. Between us, a human stands frozen, her gaze locked on my own. Heart thumping, I flap my wings.

Not yet. Not yet.

She looks from the clothing to the grey feathers on my breast, my red belly, my green back. She eases nearer, singing.

I know that melody. Her voice warbles like mine. My throat tightens and I join in, our song echoing among the trees.

Her hand reaches out, touches my back, scoops me up gently, gently. I sit in her hand, close to her wet face, my feathers aquiver. She offers a grub. Fat. Squirming. I watch it. Watch her. She swings it closer, and I take it. Swallow, and it is gone. I look for more, but she touches my head with her own, holds me there a long time. Then she lowers her hands and throws me into the air.

I spread my wings and fly.

LAST CALL

(Previously published in Silver Blade Magazine, 2018.)

MAX CROUCHED ON THE LEDGE, *muscles tight as she peered down at the plunge pool. Beside her, Sybil squatted, eyes wide. Max shot a look toward her friend, watched the rapid rise and fall of her chest, the flush in her skin. Sybil didn't belong here. Waterfall jumps were Max's thing. Sybil's comfort zone stopped high above in the clifftop picnic area, a scenic view surrounded by safety barriers and trail markers. She'd never wanted to tag along before, so why now?*

Max gestured. Are you sure?

Sybil nodded.

Max turned back toward the water and rose into position. Such a beautiful place! She breathed deep the humid, perfumed air, her body surging with electrical signals.

Then she dove.

Her arms and legs jerked inside the pod, manipulated by automated machinery even as she felt herself pressed into warming pads beneath her inclined body. Gravity had been activated, then. Mild pulses twinged her muscles again and Max stirred against the straps, licked her lips with a raspy tongue. A deep rumble, more felt than heard, chased away the last vestiges of her dreams. The sedatives must be wearing off. She lay quiet, recalling her assignment to command this maiden voyage of The Swift, first Long-Range Explorer Class ship to carry a human crew. An odd name for a ship with such a portentous mission, she'd thought at first. But when she had said as much to her C.O., he had explained the extraordinary flight capacity for that small, unassuming bird. After that, the designation made perfect sense.

Sweetened air hissed into the chamber. In the pod, a smile curled her lips, and Max opened her eyes. If Ship had awakened her, they must be close to Beyuli.

K2 2495d, her sleepy brain prompted.

Screw that. Jain had dubbed it Beyuli, like the peaceful valleys of refuge in the Himalayas back on Earth. As a moniker, that was more memorable, more meaningful. Save formality for the logs.

Months of training formed her automatic response. "Ship, I'm awake. Pod one vertical."

The capsule rotated to a standing posture.

"Ship, release restraints."

A neutral voice replied. "Bio signs normal. Acknowledge release."

Freed, Max worked in slow motion to remove her tubes and leads, then stepped out on shaky legs. An enormous yawn pulled her face into a contorted mask while shoulders and back and limbs stretched. All those endless repetitions of induced torpor and reanimation were finally paying off. The whole process felt almost natural. But Max had never been a morning person. Waking always came hard, and dregs of the torpor meds didn't make it easier. She glanced back at the warm bed she'd just vacated. Maybe another hour?

Sheesh. Wake up, Maxine. A two-year nap ought to be enough sleep for anyone, even you.

Yawning again, she scratched idly at her naked hip and took a minute to orient herself. Seven additional pods lay equidistant in a circle around the room, each accompanied by a small locker. No frills marred the grey, utilitarian space. Just like in the sims. Conditioning took over and Max slipped into her role without a second thought. She planted her earbud firmly in place.

"Ship, report." Her voice sounded weird after all this time, hoarse.

"Current ship date 21350911. Time is twelve eighteen. All systems go. Stasis pods functioning within acceptable parameters. Eleven-point-seven-zero hours to full awakening."

Max tugged on a pair of sweatpants and a long-sleeved pullover, opened a nutripac and sipped the stage-one "food" while she padded around to the other pods. Mechanical arms went about their business above the other sleepers, moving wires or adjusting restraints to ensure continued comfort but vital signs for all seven of her crew lay well within specified range. Ship was right. Ship was always right. A quick check of Swift's position showed a graphic display of their present location, still several days from Beyuli.

"Log entry, Mission Commander Maxine Patel recording. Ship has roused me on schedule. Crew is green across the board. I'll report more once I've completed my initial inspection. Conclude entry."

Max swallowed the last of her nutripac and pushed its wrapper into the recycler. A quick trip to the head, then she walked the length of the habitat module, peering into labs and storage as she went. All quiet, rooms pristine just as they'd been on launch. Soon enough these chambers would fill with bustle, a scientific crew running tests, making log entries, coming and going from the surface, playing games, talking, laughing. Too bad she couldn't have soloed on this mission. She loved her crew—good thing, since they'd be practically on top of one another for the next few weeks—but Max loved her solitude more. Too much exposure to other people, even those she liked, got on her nerves after a while. Her lips puckered.

Enjoy the peace while you can, girlie.

In the small rec room Max climbed aboard a treadmill to begin working out the kinks of long-term stasis with an easy walk. Before her, the wall bowed out in a thick plaz bubble to reveal a clear view of the star system that would be their home for the next four weeks. Below and to the left glowed the small bright arc of a gas giant crowded by tiny specs of its moons. The other biggie, an ice planet, would be in a far-side orbit now. Ahead, Beyuli hugged a tight stellar orbit along with its fellow rocky planets, indistinguishable from stars to her naked eye at this distance. To the right and above the system's plane hovered a distant blue smear of bright gas, some ancient remnant of a supernova whose designation she'd forgotten.

She was the first human being to lay eyes on this strange, alien view. Seeing it rendered in a holosim or on a star chart paled in comparison to its actual beauty. She amused herself by imagining each of her crewmembers' reactions to the sight. Seth would grunt and go back to work. Lucia and Beck, whose mathematical language sometimes required translation even among the other scientists, would at least offer helpful data like orbital parameters and equations to explain the erratic movements of this or that planetary body.

Max debated the odds and decided on projections for the other, more philosophical members. Anouk would claim this wonder for God. Jain would quote Siddhartha Gautama. Noah and Kevin would debate whether All This was created by some mythical architect, or whether the universe comprised an illusion or a test, whether authentic existence lay unseen, unfelt, as long as we wear these skins.

She scoffed. Superstitious fantasies designed to provide subjective comfort. Assigning humanistic traits and purposes to the design of astronomical gravitation and the formation of planetary systems served no reasonable goal. Why believe in something that was by its very nature beyond the realm of proof, or which had never shown scientific merit as a working hypothesis? God was a wishing well. She would rather throw her metaphorical pennies into reasonable theories.

She increased her pace on the treadmill, beads of sweat rolling down her face. Twelve hours until she could enjoy that debate. Well, probably closer to eleven now, and plenty to accomplish in the hours between. She ran through an index of tasks in her head. Test lab equipment. Double-check status of supplies (little late to realize now they were short on something). Verify status of environment suits in case of emergencies. Confirm position and progress in Control. Review inbound comms and send an arrival confirmation to Titan base. By the time the others got up, everything needed to be ready to go. She should get a move on.

Max slowed, breathing hard, then stopped and wiped her face on her shirt. Vibe shower next. She'd give a lot for a real hot-water bath right now, but that small luxury lay more than a few years in her future. She reentered the head and stripped, croaking an old rock ballad off-key at the top of her voice. Within minutes, she emerged energized and ready to tackle her to-dos.

In the lab, she unpacked equipment piece by piece, latched it all to the tables and set them on self-test. Next, she threw on a jacket, grabbed another nutripac, and walked along the aft corridor toward the shuttle bay and the engine room.

She couldn't help but wonder what they might find on Beyuli. Long-distance atmospheric scans had indicated a breathable atmosphere as well as the presence of water and, surprisingly, signs of life. Specifics remained uncertain until Swift's crew made landfall but no exoplanet closer to Earth had shown as much promise. Humanity needed a place to expand, safe from the radiation of space and climate disasters it'd brought on itself. Resource shortages had already sparked one deadly war. Max hoped it would be the last, but she held no illusions. For her crew, this mission would take just over four ship years, while fifty Earth years would pass before they returned to Titan base. That's the fastest turnaround mission planners been able to manage. Yet given the desperate state of affairs when the ship left, Max had little faith her crowded home planet would resist hostilities for that long. Even this mission had sparked tensions over who would shoulder its massive expense and whether or not the spoils of discovery would be shared equally with all. The

Swift may have been the first of her class, but unless she turned an outstanding profit, there would never be another.

So, they'd test and sample the hell out of Beyuli's air, soil and water, as well as any lifeforms they turned up—microbes probably. Drone flyovers would record holosurveys of their landing site and as much of the surface as they could manage in four weeks. If everything went according to plan, two ship years later she and her crew would be back on Titan. Another Earth year after that, they would again stand in the big conference center on base to participate in projections and plans for colonization.

Outside the bay, environment suits hung in two neat rows of five, one for each crewmember and two surpluses in case of accident or suit failure. She analyzed each one's insulation, air supply, bio- and visor displays. Next, she slid on a thermal suit and stepped through the narrow hatch into the aft passage.

Her stomach growled.

"Ship, time to awakening?"

"Nine-point-five-zero hours."

Damn. She'd taken in two nutripacs already, but her body was sucking up fuel as fast as it could. She'd grab another on her way to Control, maybe a stage-two. Her mouth watered at the thought of nearly solid sustenance.

Damn, it was cold in the main engine module. Microgravity made the going slow, but she ran every eval through to her satisfaction before pushing back to the weighted corridor. Once on a solid deck, she shed the suit and plodded forward again, stopping only to grab an edible, then headed toward Control. Ship as a whole ran big, just over three times the length of their habitable space, unwieldy enough it had required an orbital shipyard for construction. Secondary thrusters and an assortment of other mechanicals spanned out on structural supports both fore and aft, but their working and living space felt comfortable, like home. Walls in every room of the habitat module and along each corridor were soft with pale grey padding.

Recessed panels along the ceilings emitted light on either side to fully illuminate without glare. She looked around, forcing herself to consume the gelatinous ration slowly as she went. Yes, she thought. Home-ish. By mission conclusion, she would have lived aboard Swift longer than she'd been at any other domicile since she joined the military. She might even be sorry to leave when all was done.

She stepped through the hatch into Control, a shadowy chamber of dark grey everything. Fewer ambient lumens augmented the clarity of instrument panels and holo projections. Eight stations lined the module, two facing front and three on either side, each with adjustable tracseats. Straight ahead through the viewpanel lay the bulk of this star system and, hiding in the distant darkness, Beyuli.

She took another bite and dropped into the seat at her station. Every system showed normal readings, just as she'd expected. All the trepidation she'd felt during planning and training ops dropped away. So far, so good. The Swift had proven her worth.

"Ship, display a list of incoming messages."

Dozens of texts filled the screen at her station. Mission parameter revisions, updates on Beyuli's readings, notice of an apparent geothermal event on its surface and instructions to add that to her drone surveys. Only four of the incomings were visual. Max spun in her seat to face the holodisplay.

"Ship, play vids in order of receipt."

At once, a smiling, familiar form stood in the center of the module.

"Good morning!" the holographic Sybil crowed, throwing her arms wide in a long-distance embrace. Then she looked left and right, swinging her shoulder-length blond hair, and crouched closer to the camera. "I'm not supposed to be sending yet. You only just entered torpor a few days ago by my calculations and these holos are expensive! But hey, they can dock me if they don't like it. I wanted my face to be the first one you saw when you woke up."

Max grinned. That's more like the kind of rebellion she'd expect from Sybil, not waterfall diving. Not after so many close calls in air defense. They'd made a great team back then, but Sybil preferred to keep her feet firmly on the ground these days. After all they'd been through, Max couldn't blame her.

"Remember that time you snuck rum onto Titan base and Captain Mitchell caught us getting shit-faced in the supply module?" Sybil's eyes crinkled at the corners. "I still can't believe you convinced him to drink with us instead of writing us up! You always had a way of making everything sound so reasonable. No one else gets me into trouble like you did. I miss that. I miss you."

Max's smile faded. When she got back to Titan, her friend would be old, maybe even dead.

"Can't stay on long, I just..." Sybil paused. "I know how badly you wanted this. I've never been more proud of you than I am right now." She winked a blue eye, then disappeared. Max swallowed past a sudden lump in her throat.

An unfamiliar face appeared next. Black hair bunned at the nape of her slender brown neck. Frank dark gaze that met the holocam without flinching. Regulation uniform, starched and spotless. Crisp, businesslike voice with a trace of Aussie accent. How old could she possibly be? Thirty? Younger? Max wondered if they were recruiting out of grade school these days.

"Patel, I'm Ground Commander Sinclair. Commander Driskoll retired three weeks ago, so I'll be your new C.O. I've heard great things about you and your mates up there. The whole team down here sings your praises, so do us proud. Not sure what help I can be from so far away, but if you need anything, just let me know. Maybe we'll have the opportunity to meet when you get back. Sinclair out."

The third vid started, stuttered, and stopped, flickering over and over on an image she couldn't quite make out. Looked like Titan Base. Max frowned.

"Ship, check current holovid for integrity."

"Checksum invalid. File corrupt."

"Very well. Continue playback." Max took another bite from her pac. She would have to investigate that little mystery later.

The fourth sender peered out at her from a pallid face with hollow, haunted eyes. Limp colorless hair drooped around cheekbones that protruded way too far. Ragged clothing hung on the trembling skeletal frame. Behind her—it was a *her*, wasn't it?—lay Control on Titan base. Two or three people she didn't recognize rushed about the space in a frenzy.

Then the sender spoke, and the food in Max's mouth turned to ash.

Sybil?

"Max, it's true, what I said before. Worst case scenario. Everything's..." She struggled for words. "...gone. We still don't know what happened. Luna sent the probe, like I said, but..." She swallowed hard. "Earth's a cinder. Confirmed, no survivors on the planet or in atmo."

Sudden loud pounding at the door made Sybil flinch forward, her words spilling out in a confused jumble. "Luna didn't have enough supplies for survivors from orbiters and their own people, so they all came here. Eighty? A hundred people? Titan's a bigger base, they must have thought..."

Sybil's face twisted. "They were wrong," she sobbed. "We were due for resupply in another two months, but we shared with them anyway. We divvied up every last morsel, hoping... I don't know. But it wasn't enough. They've started killing us. Said they'd make what was left go farther, that they'd—"

A loud crash sounded and Sybil jumped again, glancing over her shoulder at the door, which had begun to inch open. She whirled back to the camera, her words stumbling over each other in her haste. "Doesn't matter. Even without the fighting, we can't survive without resupply. We're done. The ones they already killed are better off. Max—"

The door behind Sybil shrieked against its latches and finally gave way, spilling mutineers into the tight space. Max watched as one of them slashed a hurried blade across the throat of another crewmember just inside the door, then advanced toward the camera. Sybil thrust herself forward to fill the visual, screaming.

"Max, I was right, it's *over!* You're the last—"

The image blinked out.

Max stood less than a meter away from the projection, one hand extended toward the spot where her friend stood a heartbeat ago. She stared at the suddenly empty space, tendons in her neck stretched taut, every muscle rigid, her nutripac forgotten on the floor at her feet. Silence pounded her ears. Hair stood up at her nape. Her breath jittered in and out.

No. *No!*

"Ship." Her pinched voice sounded distant, surreal. "Replay last message."

Sybil's tortured face etched itself into Max's neurons, her scream encircled Max's heart and squeezed until every breath wheezed in her throat. When the quiet returned, Max replayed it again. And again. There had to be a mistake. Surely her friend didn't mean...

Surely The Swift's crew wasn't...

"Ship, record return communiqué."

"Recording," Ship replied.

Max opened her mouth, but no words emerged. If Sybil's message were true, if The Swift—

Max shook her head, unable to complete the thought. "Ship, belay recording. Display transmission data for all four vids at station one."

She stumbled back to her seat. The screen showed three dates.

Message one: recorded transmission, sent ED21331218.

So three days after The Swift hit speed, at least for Sybil.

Message two: recorded transmission, sent ED21411117.

Almost eight years later, Earth time.

Message three: recorded transmission, sent ED21461003.

Almost five years later.

Message four: live transmission, commenced ED21461214 at 21:20:14, terminated 21:34:42.

Live? Max blinked, looked again at the data. Yes. Live. Transmission ran much longer than the visual. Twelve years had passed on Earth since then. She scrolled through the text comms again. Nothing had come through since almost an Earth year prior to Sybil's last holo. Max struggled to grasp the revelation conveyed by her calculations. If anything had changed, someone would have sent another comm, wouldn't they?

Wouldn't they?

Oh god

oh god oh god oh *god*

Her head shook in negation. Every mouthful she'd consumed lurched in her stomach and she heaved, turning to spray the floor instead of the console.

"Spill in the control module," said Ship.

Max swiped a trembling hand across her mouth. "Noted. Ship, communications equipment has malfunctioned. Why aren't we receiving incoming messages?" She waited, expectant.

"No malfunction is detected. Communications are fully operational."

"Ship, ping Titan base. Alert me the moment they respond."

"Time required to receive response would exceed—

"Irrelevant," Max snapped. "Follow my instruction."

"Acknowledged."

"Ship, time to awakening?"

"Six point two-five hours."

Thoughts crowded her mind, blurred and disjointed. She pushed up from her chair, stepped on quivering legs over her mess and kicked the nutrient pouch on her way out of the module, every step as much on autopilot as was Ship. Max stumbled down the corridor, through the hatch into the habitat module, and kept going until she reached the viewport in the rec room. Beyuli lay somewhere ahead, a distant point of light tagged like a child's party game with all humanity's dreams. The others had yet to even see these stars. For the moment, she was the only alive and aware human in the universe.

The enormity of their situation slammed Into her like a runaway hoverbus, and she crumpled to the floor beneath its weight. Memories barged through, waterfall jumps and barrages of fighter fire and being shot down and learning to walk again. Faces and names and places and growing up in the foreshadow of social collapse and rioting in the days prior to the war. Doing bar shots with Sybil and the rest of her squadron. First impressions of Luna base, first glimpse of Earth-light, pride at her assignment to The Swift mission. Seth's body lit by candlelight in Max's bedroom, his limbs entwined with her own. Training with her crew for this voyage. Sybil's tears when she learned Max was leaving. Imagined terrors her friend endured in the lead-up to that final message.

Tears pooled on the floor beneath her face, and Max blinked away another stream, sniffed through clogged nostrils and rolled over onto her back to stare at the ceiling, reliving Sybil's last message over and over. Echoes of her screams blotted out Ship's rumble and the quiet hiss of air circulators.

Sybil was gone. Earth was gone. It was all gone.

Her stomach heaved again and she lurched to the side, retching up dregs of fluid. When it passed, she wiped a trembling hand across her mouth and sat up.

"Ship, time to awakening?"

"Five point three-nine hours."

Her arms lay leaden against her body, hands limp on the floor.

Get up, Max.

Why? What's the point?

You're Mission Commander.

Mission seems pointless now, doesn't it?

Tell that to your crew, the survivors of your species.

The crew. Fresh angst contorted her features and spilled down her cheeks. How the hell was she going to tell them? Lucia and Seth, older and more jaded than the others, would probably take it better. Anouk believed humanity was doomed anyway. This wouldn't surprise her. Noah had the Summerland to look forward to after death, but Max doubted he'd want to hasten his arrival to any afterlife, no matter how pleasant. Kevin and Beck, babies of the crew, both still bubbled over with fresh excitement for all life had to offer. How could Max bear to dim those gifted rays of light?

And Jain! Max owed her life to Jain twice over, once for her surgical skill, which pulled Max back from the brink after her fighter went down, and once for convincing her to continue with rehab when Max herself had given up. Jain and Sybil were the reasons Max landed on The Swift in the first place. After the war, Sybil and the rest of Max's squadron had gone on to pursue promising futures in the service, but Max retired from active duty and moved on. Pain of physical therapy paled in comparison to the lingering nightmares, but both eventually faded, replaced by a shiny new engineering degree and a fresh career in space, beginning on Titan.

Max loved that base! It was Titan's observatory that detected Beyuli, Titan's scientists that discerned its potential. That discovery had restored Max's hope for humanity, refueled her determination to serve, as she had in the squadron, only this time she wouldn't be destroying. She'd be setting the foundations on which they could build anew.

Except...

...except now the whole project, and all the controversy and excitement that went with it, was for naught. Swift's crew had no one left to help but themselves. If Sybil's last message were true, then Titan Base lay dead, all its humans rotting inside the structures or, if the seals had given way in all these years, frozen in a permanent state of preservation. Even if it weren't, even if some humans had managed to survive despite the odds, what the hell was she supposed to do about it? She and the crew couldn't go back—unless her ping elicited a response, no point wasting their own limited resources—so any resolution to their current predicament must be based on whatever lay ahead. She mined her considerable training for reasonable propositions to suggest a next step.

Nothing came to mind.

Max pounded a fist on her knee. What the hell could have happened? Not a natural disaster, surely nothing that would turn Earth into a cinder and kill every living thing within reach of its atmosphere. Nothing from the skies, either. A stellar event would be no mystery. Luna Base would have been affected too, maybe even destroyed. At the very least, Luna and Titan would have seen any meteor strike of extinction-level proportions long before it struck, and the result would have been highly visible.

That left only human stupidity. Probably from the same greedy mucks who ransomed Earth's food and water supplies to enslave the rest of its population. Their predilection for acting without consideration of long-term consequences had created Earth's resources dilemma and the desperate need for this mission in the first place.

Max jerked to her feet and staggered closer to the plaz. It should be those idiots who paid the price. Not the billions of innocents who died at their hands. Not her crew. Not Beck with her PhD in astrophysics by the age of 21 and 32-year-old botanist-slash-entomologist Noah and Kevin the chemist, who at age 30 was still too shy to bump uglies! They'd only just gotten a start in life. Her crew had expected to spend four years by ship-time in mission and return to a world advanced fifty Earth years. In the months of training for their trip, they'd wondered what Earth would look like when they got back. Now they'd never know.

A ragged yell tore itself from Max's throat. One hand shot out, punching the plaz bubble — a solid blow that reverberated through her knuckles and fingers, up her forearm, all the way to her shoulder.

Calm down. Think.

She swiped at her wet face and stared through the viewport as she struggled to think of a way to tell her crew. What "right" words could possibly explain that they were the last eight humans? How could she lay that at their feet?

She paced the length of the room in search of some optimistic seed. Maybe they had a reasonable shot at survival. Human history held multiple examples of population bottlenecks where recovery overcame extinction, despite the odds. One theory held that *Homo erectus* occurred as a result of speciation among a group of Australopithecina more than two million years ago. Another university study from more than two hundred Earth years ago theorized that early native populations of the pre-Union Americas descended from fewer than a hundred individuals who crossed an ancient land bridge in the north pacific. Numerous arguments had been put forth to explain limited genetic diversity in small, isolated populations over the centuries. None had been proven, but all offered feasible explanations for a set of givens in the study of mitochondrial DNA and reduced adaptability from founder effects. Clearly, *something* had traumatized the human gene pool a number of times, yet the species always managed to survive.

Maybe The Swift's crew could too.

It was conceivable that Beyuli would offer a welcoming, fecund environment devoid of any other sentient life-forms, so that her crew could spread into this new homeworld as their numbers grew. If that were so, perhaps Anouk could suggest a biological gamble Max had missed or even tweak their on-hand equipment so that they could experiment with genetic modification and expand the procreative potential of their small group. As ship's doc, Jain might know of a medical option—she'd once collaborated with a team to investigate methods of human cloning before it was outlawed. In fact, everyone on The Swift's crew was specifically chosen from the best and brightest Earth had to offer. Once Max woke the others, they could all contribute to a solution.

At the hatch, she turned back toward Control, arms wrapped around herself, tears running unheeded down her face. Even if Beyuli held sentients, perhaps she could bargain for some small space on that world where the crew could begin their new lives. Maybe the inhabitants would take them in as part of their own civilization. Cross-breeding, if it were possible, would be better than total extinction. Perhaps, in that scenario, the last eight humans could even evolve into something else. Something more.

Or maybe—

The bubble of her fantasy bumped against pointed reality, bursting into a sickening array of facts. Who the hell was she kidding? They weren't set up to colonize! That was never Swift's purpose. They hadn't the equipment or seedstock, not to mention adequate supplies. Besides, while many theories had been put forth regarding minimum numbers for viable human populations, she'd never seen an estimated low of fewer than 80-120 fertile adults. Eighty. Not eight.

And when it came to repopulating the human race, they weren't even eight. Seth carried Tay Sachs. His candidacy for fatherhood was inadvisable. Anouk, a male-to-female transexual, couldn't conceive. Neither could Jain, who had uncovered her own infertility years ago —it was the main reason she'd never married. That left Beck, Lucia and Max to bear the babies, with gay Noah and virginal Kevin to father them all. Even Max's fertility, tainted as it was by familial diabetes, had an approaching expiration date. She'd been tugging on the skirts of menopause since about a year before they left Titan. How much longer did she really have to contribute?

Five adults would never produce a sustainable population. Even if they could tweak some of the lab gear to modify the genes of their ovum and sperm—a statistical improbability—how would they implant these engineered embryos? Their medical facility was limited to simple injury repair, not fertility experiments or major surgery. Nor did they have the means even to care for healthy infants, much less incubate preemies or deal with any major neonatal emergencies.

Max found herself standing in the stasis room, staring at the pods. She tiptoed from pod to pod, staring in at the faces of her friends and crewmates, recalling moments from their shared training, celebrations of achievements, secrets and intimacies of long-term close association. If she woke them, they would quickly go from hopeful to shocked to despairing, as she'd done herself. A likely lingering death awaited, whether they stayed aboard the ship—dehydration, starvation or asphyxiation once their supplies ran dry—or went to Beyuli, where they risked a whole world of unknowns. Even barring toxins in the atmosphere or environment, predators, unwelcoming or hostile sentients who may want to kill or eat them, even if they could manage to reproduce without catastrophic results, what if they couldn't grow food there? What if their assessment of the presence of water was off by a significant percentage? What if one of them got sick or injured? She would have only prolonged their suffering, postponed the inevitable.

Rationally speaking, they may as well already be dead, so why even consider waking them? Was it for their sakes, as she'd told herself, or was it—oh ultimate quirk of fate—because Max the recluse didn't want to die alone, the last of her kind? If that was her reason, company would be selfish consolation bought at the crew's expense.

She wiped her face and wandered back out into the corridor, retracing her steps. She could reverse the awakening process, leave them in stasis indefinitely. Set the ship off in a new direction and hope that someone, somewhere, at some point in the future might find and resuscitate them. Said rescuers might even have the means to help them reproduce with greater diversity, better chances for success. Slim hope, yes, but as long as they were alive, they had a chance. Asleep, they'd burn fewer supplies. Ship could go on for years, maybe. If she left the crew in stasis and no one ever found them, they'd never know.

On the other hand, if someone *did* find the ship, a sleeping crew would be helpless. Their fate could go either way. Slim chance, true, but Max cringed at the idea of waking to a hostile situation with no opportunity to prepare or even to flee.

What, then? If she didn't want to wake them, and indefinite stasis wasn't an option, that left only...

Max's feet slowed and stopped outside the rec room.

It would be easy. Critical failure of the life support shouldn't awaken them, but just to be sure, she could modify the CO_2 scrubbers to asphyxiate them quickly, cleanly. They could then just drift away into nothingness—or into the next world of their beliefs—without ever knowing the fate of their species. Wouldn't that be kinder? Gentler? More merciful? Hadn't she, just moments ago, been decrying human selfishness?

Yes, but... kill the crew? Could she really live with herself if she did?

The irony of that question struck a manic chord and burst from her in great gasping guffaws. She bent, hands on her knees, laughing and weeping at the same time. What the hell difference did it make? If she killed them all, she'd soon follow. She remembered Death's face clearly, had held a nice long chat with it while wounded, awaiting rescue behind enemy lines. Death promised her that day they'd meet again, so Max wasn't afraid. She and Death were old friends. She wondered whether its approach would frighten the others.

Noah had told her, during one of his uncharacteristically loquacious moments, that he bought into the illusion of reality theory, that he believed consciousness creates experience. If he was right—or Anouk, for that matter, with her belief in the Catholic god—then Something or Someone awaited them at the end of the illusion, when they awakened for real. If they were right, maybe the death of humanity served a purpose.

She sobered and paced back to the viewport, wiping her face. There had to be a right answer, something she didn't yet see.

It felt wrong to "play god," as if there were such a thing. This decision belonged to the group as a whole. She had no justifiable right to decide the fate of her crew, the entire remaining human population. Except that she was the only person alive who knew the truth. And no matter what she did, she would be choosing for them all. Even refusal to act constituted a decision, so the answer really boiled down to what was most important *to her*: the theoretically possible, yet improbable chance to rebuild the human race, or one last opportunity to demonstrate compassion to those entrusted to her care.

"Ship, time to awakening?"

"Two point one-zero hours."

If she waited much longer, the matter would be decided for her.

She stared through the plaz at the alien system. It really was beautiful. She remembered her first glimpse of Earth from Luna base, and how strange Sol system looked from Titan. Constellations so clearly defined from Earth's surface fell apart out there. What a difference a new perspective made!

Max shifted and, for a second, caught a glimpse of her own reflection in the plaz. Tousled, dark hair wisped with grey framed her brown face. Traces of past laughter lined the corners of her eyes, crinkling around that small mole on her cheekbone. Seth had teased her about that spot once, after she'd told him it was a beauty mark. Grumpy old crab. Even after sex, he'd always seemed annoyed. What had she ever seen in him? Other than his physical beauty, that is, and his determination, and his underlying ache that touched her heart. Right now, the fact that he was a living, breathing human being went a long way toward validating forgiveness for *any* shortcoming, real or imagined.

Her full lips lifted Into a grin, revealing the slight gap between her top front teeth. He might be a grouch, but she loved that bristly curmudgeon with her whole heart. Indeed, she loved them all. She knew what she had to do.

Still smiling, Max left the viewport and headed down the corridor toward the stasis room.

ENDLESS POTENTIAL

(Previously published in Daikaijuzine Magazine, 2020.)

THEY ALWAYS FIND ME.

Don't get me wrong. I love my profession. But it'd be nice to have an occasional drink in peace. Disguises don't help. My skin is brown this time, my eyes grey like my hair. Still, he knows me.

He sits on the next barstool, orders a beer.

I ignore him. Stare at the telly.

"I—" he begins.

"Don't care," I say.

"—have a request."

I sip my Scotch. "Everyone does."

"You know why I'm here."

I glance at him. He's aged. More lines on his face, eyes ringed with shadows that can't be explained by years.

"I told you the last dozen times. I don't like politics."

"Yeah," he sighs. "Look where that got us."

The bar crowd roars, and I turn back to the game. The home team's star player has scored. Again. He's on a roll, that one. Three spectacular years since he and I made our deal. Four left to him, plus a show-stopping exit. A literal killer goal. He'll go out on top.

Me? I got a hundred thou and twenty-seven years in payment. It's a living.

"Did you hear what I said?" the Potential asks. His voice grates.

"Nothing's changed."

"Everything's changed," he insists. "Haven't you been paying attention?"

His urgency plucks my interest. I twist. Look him up and down. He needs a shave. Is that the same suit as last time I saw him? The same tie? His salt-and-pepper hair might be longer. Not sure.

"You look like hell," I say.

He shrugs. "Rough year."

I sip. "What do you want?"

He glances around, leans closer. "I want to unseat the incumbent."

I snort. Shake my head. "I'm no assassin."

"I didn't say kill him," he hisses. "There are other ways."

I squint. "You want to take his place."

He leans back, tucks in his chin. He didn't expect blunt, I guess. That's his problem. Subtle's not my jam. Potential takes a pull from his beer. Rubs his jaw. Nods.

"Why?"

His face contorts. "Why?" he repeats.

I wait.

A huff explodes between his lips. "Because I'm the better man for the job."

"Bullshit. You want power."

For a moment, I think he will hit me. Big mistake, that. He realizes. Changes his mind.

"I'm a damn sight better than what we've got now."

I stare at him until he looks away, fidgets with the napkin beneath his bottle, looks back.

"So, what? Your clientele is always pure of heart?"

He's got me there. Yon soccer player left a trail of offspring everywhere. Pretty sure they'll never see a dime of his money. This fine establishment's owner cheated on her taxes before *and* after I helped her land the bar in exchange for fifteen years and free drinks forever. Sam, the bartender, watered down orders on a regular basis. I helped him beat a fraud rap and took five years and a vow to never dilute my fifty-seven-year-old Laphroaig.

Still.

I want to ask Potential what changes he'll make. What he'll do different. Instead, I peer inside. See for myself. Shudder.

Better man, my ass. Potential's every bit as greedy, self-centered and indulgent as the current Big Cheese. Plots and schemes run as thick here as I'm sure they do in Head Honcho. I dunno, never met that guy. In the smarts department, though, this Potential's got it going on. Clever ideas. Plans that could work. Projects to benefit others, despite his kickbacks. A campaign to unify, rather than divide.

I'm impressed. He's no more a savior than any other politician, but on a scale of light to dark, he's a paler shade of grey.

"Won't be cheap," I say at last.

"How much?"

I sigh, sip, glance at the telly before I turn back. "Five mil advance, to start."

"That's a lot of money."

"Living expenses."

"What else?" he asks.

I purse my lips. "You're fifty-five? Sixty?"

"Fifty-seven next Tuesday."

I nod. "I'll give you eight years in office, and two years to enjoy the afterglow. The rest are mine."

"Ten—" He sputters, blanching. "That's not enough! My family—"

This is why I don't like politicians. They're all about the take, not so great on the give. I slug the last of my Laphroig, push the glass across the bar. Stand.

"Wait." His voice quavers. "Will it be a good run?"

My lip curls. "I'm your palm-reader now?"

He swallows, bar lights gleaming off sweat on his brow. "Okay."

I hold out my hand. He stares at it, looks back to my face. "No contract?"

"Don't need one."

"How do I know you'll keep your word?"

I turn toward the door.

"Wait!" he hisses, lurches to his feet. "How does this work?"

"Transfer the funds. Run for office."

"What about at the end? Do you find me, or what?"

"Don't worry about that. Just make the best of your ten years. And don't forget the money."

He shifts his weight. "What if I do?"

I smile. "Then your time's up sooner."

Potential draws a breath, blows it out. Nods.

I extend my hand again. He looks at it like it might bite.

It will.

He takes it, lifts his eyes to mine. I clamp down over his fingers, shake once, leech thirty-one years onto my own tally. His skin blanches for a heartbeat. Feels like hours. Always does.

Then it's done. His color returns. Most of it, anyway. He stands on shaking legs. "That's it?"

"It's enough."

He releases my hand and I give a little salute. "See you, Mr. President."

He frowns. Turns. Leaves. Passes a woman on her way in.

She looks around. Sees me. Starts my way.

I roll my eyes. One drink. No interruptions. Is that too much to ask?

The new Potential comes close. Hesitates. "Excuse me, Ma'am," she says. "I heard you could—"

The bartender laughs. "Another Scotch, Abby?"

I sigh. Sit. "Pour it, Sam."

———

TWENTY-NINE LANGWOOD STREET

(*Previously published in Electric Spec Magazine, Volume 14, Issue 4, November 2019.*)

THE FIRST TIME I saw her, I almost tripped over my feet and introduced my nose to the pavement. Not because she was beautiful —who could tell from the back of her head like that?—but because she occupied my bench. *My* bench. I glanced down the esplanade toward the seasonal businesses where the heady aroma of corn dogs and popcorn saturated the early summer breeze and enticed evening strollers to the waterfront. Plenty of benches sat empty there. No one had ever wanted to exchange the excitement of carnival rides and arcade games for the view of a bridge and some birds. No one except me. I get my fill of people at work every day. Moments of solitude on my bench are golden.

I shoved my hands in my pockets and passed the interloper on the bridge side, trying to check her out without being obvious. Light brown hair. Slight build. Short-sleeved dress, the sort of loose, floufy thing women wear when it's warm. Beyond her, the avenue overlooked an inlet between the mainland and the barrier island. Seabirds swooped and dove for their supper, filling the air with raspy squawks. They were the company I craved. Not some stranger. I leaned on the guardrail, resigned to a good grump, and watched the gulls.

Below the walkway on the water side, grey boulders jumbled against the seawall. Small crabs filtered the wet sand where miniature dramas played out amid much waving of claws and quick retreats into their holes at any hint of nearby movement. I raised my gaze to the waterline and sucked in a sharp breath. A rare great egret hunted amid the shallows a few yards away. I hadn't seen one of those around here in years.

"Pretty, isn't it?" the woman called.

I ground my teeth. *Add chatting to bench-stealing,* I thought, then sighed. My typical Monday irritation was not her fault. I turned, forced a smile. "Yes. Odd, too. They usually stay south of us."

"I know. This one brought me a gift." She twirled a long white feather in her fingers. "Dropped it in his hurry to eat, I suppose."

Something about her made me feel better. "I've heard egret feathers are lucky."

She nodded.

I took in her features. Delicate, almost elfin. Except the nose. That had been broken at least once. "Are you local?"

"Sort of. You?"

"Up that way." I pointed to the hill behind her. "Haven't seen you here before."

She looked down at her feather. "I used to come here a lot. I don't get out much now."

"Ah." I half-turned back toward the water.

"D'you want to sit?" She slid down and gestured to the vacated bench space.

I considered it, then joined her. "Thanks." Up close, her eyes struck a chord in me I couldn't quite define. Maybe it was their distance, even though she sat less than three feet away, or the whisper of sorrow they conveyed. Like my mom's, only grey instead of nut-brown.

The thought dredged up unpleasant memories. I planted my elbows on my knees and looked away in search of a distraction.

"Most days I come here to watch the birds. Never know what you're gonna see," I said. As if on cue, the egret rose croaking in sudden flight. We both laughed. "Case in point."

"I like them too. My husband put a wooden nest box in front of our house."

I swung my head to look at her. "Any takers?"

She brightened, a shy smile punching dimples into her cheeks. "Oh yes! Chickadees and house wrens, even a titmouse family."

"Nice," I nodded. "The best I can manage at my apartment is a window ledge feeder."

"That's fun too."

"Yeah." Maybe chatting with a stranger wasn't so bad, even on a Monday. I thrust out my hand. "I'm Joe."

She flinched. Like my mom used to. Like I used to.

"Sally," she murmured, staring at my hand.

I dropped it back to my knee. "Nice to meet a fellow bird-lover."

"Yes." Her lips parted as if she would say more. Instead, she gestured. "I should go. My daughter..."

I waited, but she stood and walked away. I watched until she disappeared into the crowd without a backward glance.

Weird. Like that egret. That's why I avoided people. Too confusing. I shook my head and leaned back, glad to have my bench to myself again.

The next evening, she was back. I rounded the bench. "Hey."

"Hey yourself," she said. She slid down.

I sat. "Been here long?"

"A while."

I looked out over the water, where the egret stalked. "I see your friend's on the prowl again today."

"Yes." Her fingers twirled the feather.

The movement drew my attention. "A new gift?"

Sally laughed, mellow music in the humid air. "If he gave me a new feather every day, he'd soon be naked."

"Good point." I watched the great white hunter a moment more, then leaned back and slouched down, stretching my legs out straight. A small groan slipped out before I could stop it.

"Are you okay?"

"Yeah," I sighed. "Too much time in a chair."

"At your job, you mean?" Her voice calmed me like soft jazz. I liked the sound of it.

"Yeah."

"What do you do?" she asked, then blushed. "I— I don't mean to pry."

I watched her fluster. "Warehouse. Order fulfillment."

"Oh. Do you like it?"

"Meh. It pays the bills." I stuck out my tongue and made googly eyes, and she laughed. "How about you?"

"Me?" Sally looked away, fidgeting, as if she'd never been asked that question before. "I'm just a housewife, a mother."

"Hardest job in the world, my mom used to say." She'd been right, at least in part, but I kept that to myself. "Don't sell yourself short."

She gave me a shy look and changed the subject.

The next two afternoons developed into a new routine for me. I didn't have many friends. Hated small talk. Never—thankfully—got invited by co-workers to their parties. The bar scene bored me. Mostly I wanted to be left alone. Thirty-one and still single, but with good reason. Relationships are like gardens. You can't grow one in the shadows. I kept to myself and never felt lonely. Or at least I hadn't. Before Sally.

After Sally?

To my surprise, I looked forward to seeing her.

By Friday, I found myself humming on my way to the bench. Sally asked about my day, and I vented about warehouse politics and coworker drama. She listened, those sad eyes conveying her empathy. I rambled for ten minutes before I noticed something felt off.

"Is something wrong?"

Her face took on a blank look. A familiar one. Hair rose on the back of my neck.

"No," she said. "Why?"

I knew a lie when I heard one. I also knew when to butt out.

Usually.

I wiped the doubt off my face, forced a laugh, and started to turn away. "Never mind. It's not my business." My own words bit like ghost peppers. How many times had others said that about mom and me?

"No! Joe—" Sally reached toward me.

That's when I saw them, blue-black finger marks stretching around her pale upper arm, just inside the short sleeve of her dress.

I recoiled, felt my face twist and my lips draw back against my teeth in an indrawn hiss. It was like passing a horrific accident on the freeway. I couldn't drag my eyes away. My mother had borne similar marks more times than I could count. We both had.

Sally snatched her hand back, wrapped her arms around herself.

"What—?" I choked. Stupid question. I knew the answer.

"It's nothing."

I wrenched my gaze up to her face. "Your husband?"

"It isn't what you think," she said with that telltale, too-casual shrug I'd seen a hundred times as a child. "I fell. He caught me before I could hurt myself. I just bruise easily."

I stared. Her words could have come from my mom's mouth. Had that story ever worked for *anyone*?

"Uh huh. Look, you have no reason to trust me. But I know what you're going through. I've been there. You don't have to live like that. You can go to the police."

She shrank from me, eyes wide. Her lips parted, their corners drawn down like she'd just swallowed sour milk. "I have to go," she murmured.

"Sally—"

She jerked to her feet and almost ran down the boardwalk.

I sprinted after her. "Sally!"

She disappeared into the evening crowd, and a flashback stopped me in my tracks...Mom and eight-year-old me disappearing into the crowd at the bus terminal. *Bus pulled out with my nose pressed to the window, panting fog onto the glass while I tried not to vomit. Dad would find us gone, I thought, chase down the bus and snatch us off. Drag us home. Make us pay.*

I shoved my hands in my pockets and ambled to the railing. A rising tide ousted the egret. Water lapped the boulders. Darting movements flickered between their bulk—crabs burrowing down for the night. My belly rang the dinner bell, but I stayed at the water-front until after dark, staring past the island toward lights like fallen stars on the sea beyond.

Sally didn't show for two days.

The next Monday, she returned. I came around the bench with a mixture of happiness at seeing her and chagrin at chasing her away. Hers was a dicey situation, especially with a kid involved. I didn't know the right thing to do, but I did know she needed a friend.

A dark sky threatened rain, yet Sally wore enormous shades, their round black lenses hiding half her face. My mom had a pair of those, too. A sick feeling brewed in my gut like the storm looming beyond the island.

"I'm sorry," I said. "I crossed a line."

Sally still held the feather, but her attention focused on something more distant than the birds. She smiled without looking at me. "I love this bench. It's almost hidden from the rest of the boardwalk, isolated without being completely cut off. It used to be my special retreat."

I frowned. "Why'd you stop coming?"

A Harley passed nearby, its thunder rumbling the air between us. After it was gone, she shrugged. "Things changed. I moved on."

I blinked, not sure what to say. She slid down, and I sat.

"You were right," she said, as if we were discussing the weather.

Her words kicked the wind out of me.

"I'm sorry," I rasped again. My voice sounded thin.

She turned. "For what?"

I kept my mouth shut.

She looked away. "I love him, you know. Despite his faults. Despite everything."

I knew all the excuses. All the justifications. My dad used to tell my mom no one else would want her. She believed him for years. "You're gonna stay."

"He's the monster I know. I tell myself it'll pass."

"Yeah," I sighed. "What about your daughter?"

This time Sally didn't reply. Gulls screeched and dove over the water, following the tide. Their cries echoed off the bridge to assault the lull in conversation. I looked down at her arm. Her sleeve hid the finger marks. Wasn't that the same dress she'd worn Friday? I frowned. I never was good on details like that.

"He doesn't like me talking to people."

Her words snatched my attention. "I don't want to make matters worse."

"Please don't walk away," she murmured at the feather. "You're the closest thing I have to a friend."

"Same here."

She managed a hint of smile. "Twenty-nine Langwood Street."

I blinked. "Excuse me?"

Her dark glasses tilted toward me with twin reflections of my confused frown. "Do you know where it is?"

"Um..."

"Out past the library, northwest part of town."

"Okay."

She peered at me a moment, those shades masking her expression. I wished she would take them off. Then she did, and I wished she hadn't. Skin beneath both her eyes shone red and black even in the gloomy light. Spots of blood dotted the sclera in the left. The right one puffed out like a balloon, closed but for a narrow slit.

"Oh," I gasped, sickened by what the bastard had done to her. Even my dad had never gone that far. One hand came to my mouth. I might have gagged.

"If I don't show for more than a day or two, you tell them where to find me."

I babbled something incoherent, still gaping at her ravaged face.

Sally slid the glasses on, stood, and walked away. I lurched to my feet to stop her, pleas crowding my throat, things I'd said to my mom. Don't go back! Let's go to the police! Stand up for yourself! But she was gone before I could push them past my lips, and they shriveled like ashes on my tongue.

A band contracted around my chest, made it hard to catch my breath. I should do something. I knew where she lived. I could report what I'd seen. Of course, if cops went to Langwood with questions, Sally might not tell the truth, especially if hubby was around. Even if officers knew she was lying, they'd have no substantial evidence to make an arrest and both Sally and her daughter would be worse off than ever.

I swallowed hard, still staring at the spot where she'd disappeared. The voices of caution and reproach argued in my head.

Walk away before you get any more involved.

But what if he puts her in the hospital?

What if he puts you in the hospital?

Screw that, I thought. Sally was a human being. My friend. No woman, no*body*, deserved that kind of abuse. Except maybe scumbags who beat people senseless. Like Sally's husband. Like my dad.

She didn't show the next day. I waited two hours. The day after, still no Sally. By the third Sally-less afternoon, experience screamed *do something*. I sat on our bench, feeling as helpless as when Dad went after Mom. Sally told me her address for a reason. Langwood Street... classy neighborhood. I'd been through that area once, when I first moved here. Big houses, large yards. Lots of space. Neighbors might not hear cries for help.

The eight-year-old in my head wanted to run back home, lock the door, pretend thirty-one-year-old me never met Sally.

I argued with myself at our bench until the boardwalk was all but empty. Stars peppered the horizon away from the city glow and the birds had long since gone to roost, but I'd decided Sally needed more than just a friend. She needed help. Like my mom had all those years ago. And I wasn't eight any more.

Just after dawn, I dragged myself from the rumpled bed, grabbed a cold shower, and called in sick at work. Then I got in my car and drove northwest.

When I got to Sally's subdivision, I began to question my sanity. What the hell did I intend to do? Knock on the door? Demand to speak to her? What if hubby answered? The last time I'd gotten between an enraged husband and his wife, I'd ended up unconscious against a wall in our dining room. I lost three molars and a portion of the hearing in my left ear that day.

I turned left onto Langwood before my mind talked me out of doing something crazy.

17...19... I drove another block. 25... 27... There—29 Langwood. I crept past, checking out the scene. The house sat atop a small rise back from the road, separated from lots on either side by woods. Stone exterior. Wraparound porch. Enormous old sycamore out front. No cars visible in the driveway, but the garage door was closed.

Then the forest tract blocked my view. I drove on, glancing at nearby homes. None were less impressive. At the end of the street, I turned around, passed Sally's once more, and parked beside the road. My inner child cringed. *What the hell are you doing?* he shrieked.

I got out of the car and locked it behind me. Mobile phone in my pocket—still there, still on—I pushed my feet onward. Birdsong filled the morning. 29's driveway approached.

I stopped, staring toward the place. An attached garage bordered the left side. A covered porch, framed by picture windows at both ends, ran the length of the house. No signs of activity. My heart pummeled my ribs as I walked down the drive. Up close I saw details blurred from the street. Escaped garden plantings ran rampant through shaggy grass. Dead limbs protruded from the sycamore's greenery. More than a few roof shingles needed replacement. The pole holding Sally's nest box, complete with crooked snake-guard, pitched like a drunken sentinel in the yard. It'd sheltered no feathered family in years. A warm breeze stirred numerous snaggletoothed wind chimes on the porch. Cracks webbed the white paint. Moss covered the lower stones on the home's exterior.

I followed the walkway and stumbled up three steps to inch toward the front door. My hovered, trembling, over the bell. For a moment, the porch blanked out, replaced by an image of my father towering over me when I stepped between him and my mother, his features distorted as he hurled insults at a *boy* who would interfere with a *man* performing his *duty*. The back of his fist on its final approach to my face. The stars of pain that had exploded in my vision upon impact. I hesitated, undecided.

Until I heard the crash.

Every part of me cringed. I cowered behind the door as though it would protect me. Muffled shouts followed from somewhere in the house. I scrambled, keeping low, to the picture window on my left. My addled brain registered nice furniture. Gauzy curtains. Thick carpet. Lots of beige. I gawked past all that to the open door beyond. Nothing.

I groped down the porch to the other window and peeked over the sill like some sleuth tracking a perp. A cushy, well-used sofa sat in the room's center, along with a pair of mismatched armchairs and, further back, bookshelves, but something closer snagged my focus. Just inside the glass, an antique table held a lacy runner, pulled askew, and framed photos jumbled out of formation. Some lay face down, one face up on the floor, its glass shattered. Beneath the shards, a posed young couple smiled for the camera. Not Sally. The woman—

Wait. Her cheekbones and grey eyes favored Sally's, though this woman's hair was red. Sally's was brown. A sister?

Another crash, closer this time, clenched my stomach and I ran. I tried to stop myself, but my legs wouldn't listen. Twice I fell. Bloodied both knees. Tore my jeans. A cold sweat broke out all over my body. My heart hammered in my throat. Back at the road, my hands shook so hard I dropped my phone twice. It seemed to take forever to press three digits to call for help. Longer for the police to arrive. Two units in black-and-whites. No lights. No sirens. They wouldn't risk squeezing the hair trigger of a domestic dispute when so much could go wrong.

I sat down the street in my car, near the cul-de-sac, watching. I couldn't see the house, but I didn't want to talk to the cops before I talked to Sally. No ambulance came. No hearse. I chewed my nails—a habit I'd thought broken years ago—and waited until the cops left with someone in the back of the cruiser.

They'd made an arrest. Good.

Five minutes after they turned the corner and disappeared from sight, I started my car and returned to Sally's driveway. This time, I pulled in close to the house. My legs still quivered on the way to the porch, this time from a different fear. My mom told more than one person to mind their own business when I was a kid. Would Sally hate me?

I swallowed hard and rang the doorbell.

I'd begun to believe she wouldn't answer when the door opened a crack, secured by the safety chain. Small help that would be if someone really wanted in, I thought.

A woman with red hair and a grey eye peered through. She looked vaguely familiar, but I couldn't see enough of her features to be sure.

"Can I help you?" she said, her words thick, forced.

"Sorry to bother you," I said. Even I could hear the tremor in my voice. "I'm Joe Smith. I'm a friend of Sally's. I just want to be sure she's okay."

The eye narrowed. "You're a friend of Sally's?"

"Yes." I cleared my throat. "We usually hang out at the waterfront, watch the birds."

The woman stared at me.

I couldn't blame her. Some stranger at her door making claims. How could I convince her? "Look, I know this sounds weird. I haven't known her very long, just a couple of weeks. But three days ago, she told me she was in trouble and gave me her address so I'd know where to find her if she didn't show for more than a day or two."

The woman straightened, an odd twist on her face. "You came here to check on her?"

"Yeah. I was, um—" I looked away and back again, "—about to ring the doorbell, and I heard some shouting, a few crashes."

"When?"

"An hour ago. Maybe two."

Her jaw went slack. "You called the police?"

I gritted my teeth. Here it comes, I thought. "Yeah. I did."

She closed the door, confirming my fear. Then I heard the chain slide out of the lock and the door opened again. That feeling of familiarity slapped me upside the head. The woman in the photo, the one with the shattered glass I'd seen in the other room right before I ran. This was her. Except her right cheekbone was flush with the beginnings of a bruise. A small cut parted her upper lip just below the blood crusted in the tip of a nostril. Three patches of blood dotted the front of her shirt. She still held a napkin smeared with rusty brown.

"I'm sorry," she said. "I don't mean to be rude. I'm—"

She stopped, blinking, but tears came anyway. I stood outside on the mat, my hands gripping one another. "Are you okay?" I asked. "Is Sally?"

She gestured and I stepped inside. She closed the door behind me and beckoned for me to follow. I frowned and matched her pace through the house to a central hall, where we stepped over broken glass and a dustpan, passed a broom leaning against the wall, and came out into the room behind the second picture window. She went to the photos table, picked up a framed shot I couldn't see from the porch, and handed it to me.

Sally. Same brown hair, same sad grey eyes. Same dress she'd worn on the boardwalk that first day. I looked from the photo to the woman and back.

"People always told me I looked like her," she said, "except for the hair. I got that from my dad."

"Your dad."

She nodded. "I'm Celia Collins. Sally Jameson was my mother."

"Celia," I parroted. I shook my head to clear it. "Is Sally okay?"

"Mr. Smith," Celia said, a small wrinkle between her red eyebrows, "my mother is dead."

I felt like I might pass out. "I'm too late, then. I should have come right away, the first day she didn't show at the park." I pushed one hand through my hair, pulled my lips back against my teeth. "Damn it. I should have—"

"No, you don't understand." Celia stepped closer. "She died a long time ago, twenty-three years today, as a matter of fact."

Her voice pelted my ears in a muted echo, as if funneled through a tube. I shook my head. What was she talking about?

"You look a little pale." Celia laid a hand on my arm. "Come. Sit." She led me to an armchair in the center of the room.

"What... I don't..." I stammered. "I'm not...Why would Sally—" I looked up at Celia's face, at the bloom of purple spreading up the side of her face and creeping under her eye. Understanding crept closer.

"Like mother, like daughter," she said. "Except I didn't die."

"Your father killed her," I said. Was that *my* voice?

"Yes," she whispered.

"How old were you?"

"Eight." She looked away, picked at a fresh tear on her khaki slacks. "He beat her to death while I hid in the closet. I thought he'd kill me too."

"I hope he went to prison." My rancor fell hot from lips too familiar with the feel of cuts and bruises.

"No," she whispered. "He shot himself."

I felt my face twist at that. Too quick an end. I gestured at her cheek. "Your husband?"

She nodded. Her lips worked, but no sound emerged.

"Yeah," I sighed. "Abuse runs in families." I should know. I'd researched it long enough to know I was more likely to abuse a spouse than other guys.

A choked sob caught her off-guard and she folded in the chair next to mine. Time distorted, stretched thin as a veil while she cried herself out. I waited until she wiped her face and sat up before I slid my open hand forward—slow, easy, no sudden moves—palm up, an offer of support. Celia took it, squeezed it, then let it go.

"I don't know how you knew," she croaked. "If you hadn't—"

"Not me." I shook my head. "Your mom did this." I looked down at the framed photo in my other hand, at Sally's practiced smile. "Will you tell me about her?"

Celia and I talked for a couple of hours before I drove home and parked on the hill. Any other weekday, I'd already be at the waterfront by now with my new friend. I got out and shuffled down the hill to our bench.

Empty.

I stared at it a moment. It felt wrong to sit there now. Instead, I swung my gaze to the inlet without really seeing it. The air hung damp, salty with high tide. Shrill cries rang in my ears, calls from the ever-present gulls. The view from our bench. An everyday familiar setting. Except everything felt surreal. It would never be the same. It couldn't.

I slumped, shoulders hunched forward, hands slack at my sides, a lump in my throat. Every word Sally had said to me replayed in my head, followed by stories from Celia's memories until a shimmer of movement caught my eye. I froze, gooseflesh stampeding down my arms and up the back of my neck as I watched the sleek white feather drift past my face and land at my feet.

I tore my gaze away to search the sky and the water's edge.

No egret today. Just this gift. I picked it up and my fingers closed around the feather's shaft, twirling, twirling.

Maybe it would be okay to sit here after all. Just for a little while.

SWITCH

(Previously published in Aphotic Realm Magazine, 2018.)

JELLO SMACKED Benny in the back of the head, stray droplets splattering in orange beads that jiggled against the inside of his glasses. Benny gasped and spun, almost losing his tray, to face his assailant. Stupid brat! The boy pointed, laughing, while his mother shook a finger.

"Now Philip, I told you not to throw your food," the brat's mother chided.

Gobbets of goo oozed through Benny's thick brown hair and dribbled beneath his collar to slide in sticky trails down his back. He ground his teeth, ignoring the cacophony of a mad Friday night, and stared daggers at table six before taking two steps toward the boy seated there. "You—"

Saul, the manager, materialized out of thin air with his shiniest customer-service smile.

"Is there a problem here?" he asked.

"It took us half a goddamn hour to get our food," blurted the man, "and when we finally got it, the crap was cold."

"So sorry about this," Saul mewled at the customers. "We'll get you a fresh meal, on the house."

"But—" Benny blustered.

"Kitchen," hissed Saul. "Now."

The moment the door swung closed behind them, Benny sat the tray down with a clatter.

"Half an hour, Benny? What the hell? They're regulars! You gotta give them some priority!"

"They're regular pains in my butt! That little shit's always making trouble—he threw Jello at me, Saul!"

"It happens. Clean it up and move on."

Benny swallowed his next words. Saul didn't want to hear that his "regulars" took fifteen minutes to make up their minds in the first place or that their darling offspring spat at him when he first approached the table. Being right wasn't worth losing his job. Twelve years of service or not, he could be easily replaced. His shoulders slumped closer to his chest than usual.

"I need a couple minutes to get this mess out of my hair."

Saul jerked his head toward the men's room, then barked at the cook.

Benny locked the door and looked at himself in the mirror. The hair net had been no protection against the brat's attack, and he pulled it off and dropped it on the sink. Wet paper towels only went so far toward a jello spill. He did the best he could. Cleaned his glasses. Wiped his sticky hair. Scrubbed away the orange spots on his hollow cheeks and slender neck. He unbuttoned his uniform to glance at the orange trails that gleamed between his jutting shoulder blades, but he couldn't reach those. They'd have to wait. With a sigh, he settled the hairnet and straightened his clothing and finished his shift in a stiff shirt.

Probably would have been a good idea to shower before hitting the pub, but if he went home, he wouldn't go out again. No way was he missing his weekly drunk, not after a day like this one. Friday night at O'Malley's made the rest of his week bearable. Patrick would pour him a Ten High and ask about his week. Benny would complain and bemoan dropping out of school. Then they'd surrender their meager conversation to some game on the telly. Benny would drink himself numb. Patrick would put him in a cab. Tomorrow he'd wake up and start over. The dance never varied.

At the subway station, and in the car, fellow travelers stood or sat apart from the greasy, sticky smell of his uniform. Benny didn't notice. At his stop, Benny pulled himself off the train car and trudged through the heat to the welcome coolness of the pub. Inside, the smell of stale sweat and cheap booze wrapped him in a familiar cocoon and Benny smiled for the first time that day.

"Hey Patrick."

The bartender nodded. "'Sup, Benny. How ya been? Good week?"

"Same ole'."

"Yer usual?" Patrick asked, his hand already reaching for the bottle.

"Yeah."

Patrick nodded, poured, and slid the glass onto a napkin.

Benny claimed a stool, looking around. The predictable suspects filled booths or played pool, men and women with familiar, lined faces whose lips pulled down at the corners under the weight of drudgery. A few, like him, manned the bar, including one stranger. Slim man. Dark hair with wisps of grey at the temple. Tallish. Long clean-shaven face. Snappy dresser. New Guy oozed more enthusiasm from his bar stool than Benny ever felt, even on a good day. Patrick could run his whole bar off that surge of energy.

"What's that fruity smell?" Patrick asked, his nose wrinkled.

"Orange jello," Benny said, sharing his run-in with the Brat from Hell.

"Oi! That bites," Patrick said, shaking his head. Another customer called for a refill and the bartender excused himself.

"Waiter, huh?" New Guy said.

Benny shrugged and downed half his whiskey. "Yeah."

"My hat's off to you. Not sure I could do that for a living."

"A living." Benny snorted. "Is that what they call it?"

"Falls short of the brochures, does it?"

"You could say that." Benny knocked back the rest of his drink and signaled Patrick for another. "Not sure which one is worse."

"Which what?"

"Which job."

"You have more than one?"

Benny nodded. He gulped his booze, face twisting at the burn. "Two," he rasped.

"Waiting tables and ..."

"Parking attendant."

The stranger nodded, bar lights reflected in his eyes. "Reaching for the stars, aren't you?"

Smartass. "Yeah. Well, it pays the rent."

Three glasses later, New Guy had moved closer and introduced himself as Dave and joined in with his own blues tune. It's true. Life sucked for the little guy. Work yourself to death to make ends meet, and no chance to break even, much less get ahead, but his words rang false. The way Dave dressed, the way he carried himself made Benny wonder if this guy had ever known real hardship.

Benny signaled Patrick for another round. "Every morning, I wake up, shower, eat breakfast, drink a cuppa coffee and hop the train so I can sit for eight hours in a tiny booth in a smelly garage and take crap from people all day. I'm bored out of my mind. In the winter it's cold. In the summer it's an oven. Then I jump another train to wait on jerks who throw food at me or stiff me on tips. What for? I mean, yeah, I'm paying my bills, barely, but what's the point?" He stared at the space behind the bar, shaking his head. "Sometimes I wonder is this all there is. You know?"

"Yeah," Dave said. "I do."

Something in his tone caught Benny's attention and he turned to find an odd expression on his new bar pal's face. The light in the man's eyes gleamed brighter. How was that possible?

He blinked, shook it off. "I'm just so tired. I don't think I can do this much longer."

Dave's lips twitched. Not a smile, exactly. Not a smirk, either. "This is where I'm supposed to say, 'Come on, man, suck it up, it won't always be like this.'" He peered at Benny. "Is that what you want to hear?"

"No," Benny grunted. "Don't be just another sap who feeds me bull, Dave. Because then I gotta ask—when's it gonna change? Huh? Tomorrow? Next week? Next year? I got no prospects. No schooling. No training. This is as good as it gets for me, and it's not enough. Not nearly enough."

An odd intensity crept into Dave's expression, his eagerness reaching across the space between them to raise the hair on Benny's arms. Benny blinked, squinting at him in the dim light.

"Then what do you want?" Dave pressed.

"A winning lottery ticket." Benny turned away from the challenge.

"I'm serious."

There was that tone again, the one Benny had heard in Dave's voice earlier. Benny looked back at his bar pal. "So am I. One single, sole-jackpot-winning lottery ticket would solve a lot of problems for me."

Dave's silence stretched out, his eyes demanding a better response until Benny squirmed on his stool.

"It would!" he insisted, defending himself even though Dave hadn't said a word. "I could quit both my jobs and do things I never got a chance to do before. I could stop living from one dead-end job to another. Make a real life for myself."

"What kind of life?"

"I dunno," Benny said, waving an arm in a vague gesture. "Something more exciting. If I won the lottery, I'd always have plenty of money, maybe a girlfriend, a chance for some down time. I'm tired of being a lackey, ya know? That kinda money grants a man a whole new level of importance. People listen to him, do what he says."

"So, you want to be a boss."

Benny thought about it. "No. I'm sure that has its perks, but it's gotta have a lot of responsibility, too."

"What, then? Forget about the lottery for a minute," Dave urged. "If you could pick any life you wanted, what would it be?"

Benny chewed on the possibilities while Patrick refilled his glass.

"I don't even know what options are out there. I've never seen anything except the bottom of the heap," he said, almost to himself. "I'd definitely want a job that paid better, a nicer apartment. But that's not the most important thing."

Dave leaned forward, his eyes fastened on Benny's face. "What is?"

"Power." Benny drank. "I'd want a life where I could call at least some of the shots. I've been a nobody my whole life. I'd pick a life where lots of people knew who I was, so when I came in the door, all conversation stopped."

"Like a movie star?" Dave sounded almost disappointed.

"No, jeez, not like that. I'd want to be that guy people don't screw around with, the guy with the cajones and the resources to get even with everyone who screwed him. Me, Benjamin Noah Swann. I'd like to be the guy people go out of their way to make him happy, to take his coat or fill his drink." He grinned a little, warmed by the booze. "I'd make people quake in their boots."

Dave huffed, as if unbelieving. "So, you'd give up all this," he gestured, "to be a big shot tough guy."

Benny stared at him. Dave's words sent a crawling sensation through Benny's gut, but the attraction of the game they'd been playing sparkled like starshine in the grunge of his life. He nodded.

"Yeah. I would."

Dave smiled, his features oozing into a look of satisfaction that shriveled Benny at the edges. Dave lifted his glass. "Then let's toast the miracle that will make that happen, my friend."

"That I can drink to," Benny said and drained his glass.

~

He could never say, later, what woke him. A change in temperature or air pressure. A slight sound. Rustling of clothes.

His eyes snapped open in the darkness to see movement above him, and he rolled away fast. Something large slammed into his pillow. He kept rolling, his body on autopilot for a light landing on the far side of the bed. Whirling, he met the next attack face-on, hands raised to grab the swinging bat before it could make contact with his head. Instead of trying to free the weapon, he shoved its horizontal mass as hard as he could, felt the impact smash his assailant's face, heard the guttural grunt of pain. His foot shot out to hook behind the intruder's uncertain stance, then he shoved again. The shadow before him went down and he leapt forward to straddle it, shoving the bat—*his* weapon now—against the gasping throat. Hands slapped at his face and arms and knees, clawing at his fingers to rip them away from the choking wooden throttle. He leaned in, threw his weight into the effort. The panicked body beneath him bucked and kneed him in the back. He rode out the frenzy, his heart pounding as if it would batter its way through his ribcage and join the fight. It didn't matter who this was, only that they never do this again. The moment the struggles ceased, he grabbed the head and twisted. A short, sharp snap reverberated in his ears and echoed back from the walls.

He sat atop the corpse letting his breath return to normal before he stumbled to his feet and staggered back against the bed. What the hell just happened?

He just murdered a guy. That's what.

He'd never harmed a flea before, though he had entertained spiteful thoughts about that bratty kid in the diner. His body began to shake, and he ran a trembling hand over his face before his brain spoke up in defense of his actions. Yeah, he killed someone. An intruder. It was self-defense, wasn't it? And anyway, how did someone get into his flat in the first place? How had he even survived an attack like that? He'd never been a fighter, or trained in martial arts, unless you counted balancing two laden trays while crossing a crowded dining room without dropping or spilling anything. So how had he been able to snap someone's neck for chrissakes?

Whatever, it didn't matter. He should call the police. He shook off his confusion and felt his way through the room to the nightstand to retrieve his glasses and his phone. Fumbling in the dark, he switched on the bedside lamp—

—and stopped cold, thumb frozen over the phone's keypad.

This was not his phone. In fact, this was not his bedroom. He'd never seen this place before. Where the hell was he?

He dropped the phone on the bed and flipped the switch by the door. Light flooded the room and he stared at his surroundings. Muted purplish walls punctuated by real honest-to-god paintings, acres of floor carpeted in dark grey, silk sheets pulled off onto the floor, piles of pillows on the bed, floor-to-ceiling drapes, heavy wooden furniture.

Body on the floor, its face a bloody mess.

His feet carried him through the surreal space toward the far end of the room where a door stood ajar, an invitation to explore. It swung open with nary a squeak, and he flipped on the switch.

A stranger stood silent in the bathroom, and he flung himself back out into the bedroom, ducking and whirling to face this new threat. But no one came, and he crept back toward the door, every muscle tensed and ready to fight.

No sound. No movement. His blood pounded so loud in his ears he thought the new intruder might hear. Agonizing seconds passed before he shot a look into the bathroom.

Nothing.

He risked a more detailed look. The room was empty. He stood and reentered to see the stranger again—his own reflection.

His gaze locked on the image. One hand came up to touch the

stubbled, bald pate, the firm cheeks and thick neck, the mustache and small patch of hair below his bottom lip. The scar on his forehead.

Benny did not have a scar on his forehead. Nor, for that matter, had he ever looked this good in silk boxers. "You must work out," he muttered at the mirror, where the stranger's lips moved to the same words. It wasn't him. Except—it kinda was. The eyes were almost the same. They looked strange without his glasses, which he didn't seem to need. The cheekbones were familiar. Ditto face shape. He pulled down the boxers to inspect the package. Yep. That was his equipment. Damn. Everything else was improved. Why not that too?

He snapped the boxers back into place, looked at his face, turned his head to one side, then the other. He raised a hand. The stranger did the same. He barked a laugh at his own weirdity, but how was he supposed to react to this situation?

New bedroom. New body. "What else is different?" he whispered at the reflection.

He turned back to the room, exploring. A second door opened on a closet almost the size of his old flat. He could explore that later. The third door led to a narrow hallway, same grey carpet, same muted purple walls. To one side he found another lavatory, to the other an office. Later, he thought. Lay of the land first.

The other end of the hall ended in a king-sized great room filled with expensive furniture, more paintings, and company. An Hispanic man in a dark suit stood, hands clasped before him, by the main entrance. Another, smaller man in tailored clothing stood before the hearth. Hands in his pockets, he examined the nude portrait above the mantel. Some instinct brought his attention to the hallway.

"Benjamin. Good. Glad to know you're still on your game. I was beginning to worry." The man's lips curled in a smile that did not reach his eyes.

Careful, Benny. You are on foreign ground here. "So, this was a test?"

The stranger shrugged. "You've always been good, Benjamin. One of the best I've ever seen. You never make a mistake. But your

last job turned into such a colossal fuckup, Joe here had to run inter-
ference for you. If the great Jammer's lost his touch, I need to know."

"Right." Benjamin. Jammer. Not Benny, then. Not here. Which
was....where, exactly?

"Joe," the man said, "take out the trash."

"Sure thing, Mickey." Joe opened the door and spoke to another
man outside who came in and disappeared into the bedroom with a
small shoulder bag.

Mickey ran a hand through his immaculate white hair and took a
seat in the wing chair nearest the fireplace. "I want to give you a
chance to regain my trust."

"I'm listening."

"Nolan Whitehall," Mickey said. He pulled a photo from his
breast pocket and stared at it. "Been doing my laundry for years,
keeping my books audit-ready."

Jammer waited. The third man came back out of the bedroom,
satchel over one shoulder, wrapped body over the other, and exited
out the front. Joe closed the door behind him.

"Turns out he's skimming." Mickey dragged his gaze to Jammer's
face and held out the photo.

Jammer took it. "You want me to talk to him?"

"No. I want you to plant him. Boy used his warning chit last
time."

Mickey was watching. Jammer didn't think the man would miss
the smallest twitch. "No problem."

"In fact, do them both."

Jammer's heart skipped a beat. He willed his face to remain
neutral. "Both?"

"Him and his wife." Mickey grinned. "Sends a stronger message."

"Got it." Jammer swallowed in a dry throat.

"That's not going to be a problem, is it?"

"Nope."

"Good. You won't get a second test." Mickey got to his feet and
headed for the door. "Address is on the back of the picture."

The door clicked shut behind Mickey and Joe, and Jammer crossed the room to lock it behind them. Not much of an assurance, but he'd take what he could get right now. He hurried to the bedroom. Not even a trace of blood darkened the carpet.

So, no need to call the police then. Probably wouldn't be the smartest move anyway. Mickey would not approve.

He sank down on the edge of the bed, staring around the strange room, then pinched himself hard on the inside of his thigh.

Ouch! Not a dream. He replayed the ordeal, recalled how it felt to handle himself so well. Benny wouldn't have known how to do that thing with the bat even if his life depended on it—which it had.

Jammer had known, though.

I'm not Jammer. But he *was* in Jammer's body. It had filled in where his memory could not. How—

A memory flashed in his head—a clear image of his conversation with Dave in the bar. *I'd want to be that guy people don't screw around with.* Hell, maybe Dave was like the poor man's tooth fairy, because Benny sure got his wish. He hoped he wouldn't come to regret that conversation.

Never mind. Far more important right now to get acquainted with his "host." If he planned to live long in this whatever-it-was, he'd need information. Jammer lurched to his feet and began going through the bureau. From there, he progressed to the closet. Then to both bathrooms. The front room. A small gym. The kitchen. Jammer's tastes ran to the expensive, and from the looks of things, he cooked. A lot. He'd never seen such a well-equipped kitchen outside a restaurant in his old life.

He saved the office for last. Its simple, uncluttered space told him a lot about the man whose skin he wore. Jammer liked things crisp. Efficient. Simple. A computer on a glass-top desk, a matching credenza, a couple of chairs, and a sculpture in the corner that bore vague human resemblance.

Oh, and the painting. Sheesh. The closest thing to a painting Benny ever owned was a poster from a long-ago Flock of Seagulls concert set in a plastic silver frame. Jammer must be a patron of the arts.

No file cabinet. Everything had to be stored in the computer then, no doubt double- or triple-protected. Jammer gritted his teeth. Computer security wouldn't bow to muscle memory. He'd have to know the password.

Moving around the desk, he dropped into the chair. The computer screen came to life, a plain black prompt on a white screen.

"Optical scan: Ready."

Okay. Where's the scanner? Nothing sat atop the desk but the computer. Maybe....

He leaned forward, his face a few inches from the screen. From the top of the frame, a small red light probed his right eye, and the screen changed to a black background with three unlabeled icons. Jammer kept his computer as tidy as the rest of the place. Invoices, monthly bills, vehicle registrations all filed by year/month/date, storage locker address and inventory of weapons. It was almost too easy. After another few hours, he'd learned much info necessary to carry off this new identity.

Now he just needed to figure out how to kill someone. Outside the whole fighting-for-his-life scenario, that is.

He leaned back in the chair. Could he really do it? Yeah, he'd just rammed a man's nose up into his brain and crushed his windpipe and then—for good measure—snapped his neck, but that was self-defense. This job for Mickey would be murder, plain and simple. Could he do it? More to the point, did he have a choice? Given the recent interview with his new boss, Benny—no, *Jammer,* he was Jammer now—doubted Mickey would take "no" for an answer.

Maybe he should leave town, grow his hair out, change names.

Yeah. *That* would end well. Mickey didn't seem the type to let him go easily. Jammer didn't want to spend the rest of his life running.

He got up and opened the drapes to peer out at the night skyline. Chicago. Huh. Strange. He'd switched bodies, lives, and jobs, but his city was the same. He'd have to check out the diner and O'Malley's, see if they were different too. Hell, his new job might even take him to those places, or to others from his previous powerless life. He imagined walking up to Saul to tell him off, or even getting him fired. Let him see how it felt for a change. But before he could do any of that, he had to handle this job for Mickey. Jammer hoped it would come as easily as the fight with the bat.

He went back to the great room and snatched up the photo of his target. Nolan Whitehall. White guy. Blond ponytail. He looked about as tough as any other accountant. Jammer looked down at the layers of muscle in his own arms and shoulders, his taut belly and sculpted legs. Oh yeah. He felt sure he could take the man. Would Whitehall be afraid? Would he beg for his life? For his wife's?

A spark of excitement lodged in Jammer's gut and crept, quivering, through his body. Finally, it was his turn to be the big shot. No more putting up with rude customers. No more spitting brats. No more jello in his hair. That was Benny's lot. He was Jammer now, and Jammer took no shit.

He carried the photo into his office and dropped it on the desk. He'd need to visit the storage unit tomorrow, see his tools for himself, maybe take one of the handguns to a range and test his skill. Surely even this finely tuned body had limits. He needed to know what they were. He couldn't afford to screw it up.

~

The fork caught him in the ribs hard enough to draw blood, and Benny winced, dropping the tray. Food sprayed in all directions, painting a spectacular mosaic of color and texture across the floor, as well as every nearby patron.

"What the hell—" Benny babbled. He peered through thick glasses at his new surroundings. Christ on a pogo stick—a *diner*? He'd traded his upscale racket for a waiter gig? Oh no. No no no. This would not do. No way he'd wait tables. Uh uh. Even Jammer wouldn't last a week in this hole. Maybe Mickey wasn't so bad after all.

Beside him, the demon-spawn child only pointed and laughed, fork still clutched in one hand. Benny glanced at the blood on his shirt before he snatched the brat by the shirt to hang mid-air, inches from Benny's face.

"If you ever do that again, I'll squash you flat," he whispered.

The brat bawled. The mother screamed. The father came out of his seat, fists balled and ready. Benny dropped the kid and swung at the father with an unfamiliar, scrawny arm that threw the punch too wide.

Saul materialized amid the squawks of angry patrons and screaming kid and threatening father. "What happened?" Saul asked, his voice calm, controlled.

"This bastard attacked my kid and then took a swing at me!" the father blustered. "You'll be hearing from my lawyer!" He picked up his boy, gestured to his wife and started toward the door.

"Hold on," Saul consoled. "There's no need for that. Let us fix this."

Father jabbed a finger at Benny. "He's a maniac! I'm not bringing my family anywhere near him again."

"You're right." Saul turned. "Benny, you're fired. Get your things and get out."

An ugly snarl twisted Benny's features and he thought—hard—about going after the brat's dad. Instead, he forced his face into a blank mask. "Fine. I don't need this shit."

He shoved his way out the door and stormed down the sidewalk. He hadn't meant to lose it like that. It was the fork that did it. And the shock of his new status. A waiter. He grunted. He'd done a job for Mickey last month, just two blocks from here. This whole neighborhood was a dive. Not to mention his back and feet ached. No thanks. This wasn't at all what he signed up for.

Just ahead, he glimpsed a familiar form through the crowd.

Shoving others out of the way, he rushed forward to grasp the man's shoulder and spin him around.

"Dave!" he cried with relief. "Am I glad to see you! Listen. This isn't going to work. I've changed my mind."

Dave smiled. "Benny, it's a one-time thing. You knew that when you made the deal."

Benny pushed his glasses up on the bridge of his nose and barked a nervous laugh. "Yeah, but you didn't explain that I'd still be a lackey."

"We're all lackeys, Benny. It's just a matter of degree."

"Stop calling me that. My name's Jammer."

"Not here, it isn't."

"But," he began, then stopped. "This isn't what I expected. I mean—look, does this Benny loser even have money? Assets? Anything I can use to make this deal worthwhile?"

"No."

"Then I want out."

"*You* sought *me*, Benny. You paid for an anonymous life, away from Mickey and his people. A risk-free identity where you weren't always looking over your shoulder. Your words, Benny. I gave you what you asked for. Now nobody's more anonymous than you."

"No. I can't live like this. I won't."

Dave shrugged. "You can't undo it, either."

Benny's blood pressure ticked up a dozen notches. "You don't understand," he said, stepping closer. "I'm not asking. I'm telling. Send me back."

"Sorry."

Benny's punch, when it flew, felt spot-on. Dave caught it with one hand and stopped it cold. Still smiling, Dave shook his head. "Shouldn't have done that, Benny."

The two men stared at one another before Dave released Benny's fist and whirled, stepping out between parked cars to cross the street.

Benny watched him go through a sizzling red haze. People didn't just walk away from him like that. He wasn't some wuss that could be pushed around, like this Benny fool he'd switched with. He was Jammer.

Time to inspire some fear.

Jaw set, Benny followed Dave into the street.

He never felt the impact of the bus, nor that of the car where his body finally landed in macabre, tangled array. He never heard the screams of nearby pedestrians or the screeching of brakes. He didn't see Dave watching from the opposite curb, or the horror on the faces of surrounding drivers. Limbs twisted, eyes open, mouth ajar, Benny stared over his shoulder into a clear blue sky. He never saw that either.

~

The bus travelled another fifty feet after the driver, Nolan, stood on the brakes. Holy shit—where had that guy come from? Oh this was *just* what he needed. After the week he'd had....

Nolan threw the bus into park, pulled the hand brake, and fell forward over the wheel, oblivious to the chaos around him as he wept.

Great move, Whitehall, he thought. He never should have asked for that deal.

UPDATE

THIS MORNING, I wake with an urge to kill and a foolproof assassination plan in my head, which is odd, given that my usual occupation is gardener.

As soon as I recognize the conflict, I call the helpline, grab my clippers, and stand at my kitchen table pulling fresh flowers from a vase. Snipped blossoms, stems, and leaves grow into a map, the layout for my attack, while I wait.

"Universal Management," the receptionist says. "How may I direct your call?"

"Hi." I scan the plan's configuration for blind spots. "Tech support, please."

"Happy to help. Which department?"

"Human. Misdirected updates." No, that pillar in the parking garage is farther north. I nudge the vase in that direction.

"I'm sorry, there is no such department at Universal Management. Maybe someone in Human Software could help?"

"That depends." I push a rosebud along the passage my mark will take later today. "Can they correct an erroneous overnight update?"

The long pause at the other end of the phone draws my focus away from the tabletop mock-up. "Hello?" I say. "Is anyone there?"

"Sorry," another pause, "but I think you may be confused. Universal Management updates always go where they're supposed to."

I huff the kind of laugh that catches you unaware when you're being told you are mistaken, and you know you aren't. "Then maybe I was hacked. Who do I speak to about that?"

The receptionist transfers me to a customer service tech, who takes my name, listens to my complaint, and puts me on hold. I lean on my hands, peering down at the white Formica table. The target will be at his most vulnerable *there*, at the turn onto Main Street. I'll be onsite early, anyway, to oversee the botanical details for today's parade. Ubiquitous security might make this hit tight, but I've pulled off more challenging projects before.

Haven't I? I squint.

Oh. Never mind. That was the overhaul of the botanical gardens. Definitely harder than taking out this mark.

A new voice comes on the line. "This is the division manager. You're Jaqueline?"

"Please, call me Jaq." I break off a piece of sorrel to serve as a place marker in my layout and nibble on the rest. Bruised leaves ooze lemony juice on my tongue.

"Very well, Jaq. What seems to be the problem?"

"I think I got the wrong update last night."

Condescending laughter meets my claim. "I'm afraid that's not possible."

"Then explain to me why I went to sleep last night as a master gardener and woke up this morning aimed at a...non-gardening job?" I snip stalks and foliage from Shasta daisies and add them to the table's eclectic map.

"Our system is infallible. Trust me, you got the update intended for you."

"I'm not so sure. My usual job involves things like renovating the Italian garden downtown last spring. Or ordering four hundred pounds of white rose petals for President Shubert's procession this afternoon."

The DM hesitates. "And which update *did* you receive?"

"All the intel for a job as far from gardening as you can get." I fan rosemary sprigs in a wide arc to serve as the sweeping entry of the International Building downtown where I'll join the parade later today, assuming this mix-up isn't rectified by then.

A sigh wheezes through the phone. "All right. Let me double-check. Can you verify your identification?"

"Zed 34 Niner 575 Alpha."

"Hold please."

The botanical map morphs in my head to a visual of the street where my floral plans are already being set up. The President's secretary left the details in my hands, and I've gone all out. Garden staff dressed in immaculate white uniforms with matching boutonnières. The parade route lined with tall potted topiary. Floral baskets in sprays of white blooms hung from every lamp post. Verdant garlands with fresh gardenias draped along the route to keep the crowds back from the street. Rose petals preserved and bagged already sit in the dispersal vehicle, where I'll ride a dozen meters ahead of the Prez's car while I sit with an aide in the back and shower festive white blossom bits on the street. As if the Prez is some virgin sacrifice being led to the slaughter.

All that remains is to time my "cough" perfectly so that the dart will find its mark and the toxin can begin its work before anyone notices my movement. Normally, I'd say that's a real gamble. I've never handled a weapon. After this update, though, I feel like I was born with a trowel in one hand and a gun in the other.

The phone clicks. "Director Smith here." His voice is deep. Rich and velvety like a thick bed of black pansies. "What seems to be the problem?"

I blink. "Director *Robert Alan* Smith? From the Philadelphia office?"

"Yes." He pauses. "Have we met?"

My latest update snaps this final puzzle piece into place, Smith's voice giving yesterday's recommendation to raze the botanical garden —the one I redesigned—and build a resort in its place.

That's *my* garden.

Map and plan coalesce in perfect symmetry. The scene flashes through my newly enhanced mind. Smith riding in the back of the convertible limo behind us, towering beside the shorter Prez on the raised back seat. Smith's square-jawed profile turning toward the crowd on his left and exposing his jugular. My throat tickles with the urge to cough.

"Not yet." A smile fattens my cheeks.

He hesitates. "How can I help you, Jaq?"

"You know, it's nothing. I've resolved the issue myself."

"You're sure?" He sounds relieved. "Universal Management wants all our citizens to be happy."

"I'm positive, Director Smith. Thanks for your time."

"It's my pleasure. You have a nice day."

"Goodbye, Director Smith." I touch *end*, make one final adjustment to my map, and step back with a smile. I won't think of it as an assassination.

I'm just a gardener pulling a weed.

MURDER OF CROWS

(Previously published in Entropy Mag, 2019.)

I'M AMAZED, really, this bench don't have a dip where my arse has pressed against it twice a day, seven days a week, for so many years now. Back when they installed this new one after the old seat began to splinter, I had to find a new spot until the workmen got done. My birds didn't like that. They're fond of routine, my sweeties. I know I shouldn't cater to them, but I can't help it. I love 'em so! I'm like my da' in that, I suppose.

I'm late today, and they're already waiting. There, in the oaks and elms. See? Those black swaths atop the branches? Yes. Here they come! Two. Three. A swarm.

A murder.

I always laugh at that. Such an odd term for a group of crows! They're playful, yes, and they might bite if you poke 'em. But mostly they want food. Or toys. I bring shiny trinkets from time to time, though it's been a while. I guess they're due.

"Come on, then," I call to them, and they do. Out comes my bag.

I remember when it was a small pouch of seed. Now it's a paper sack full of mix—fruit, nuts, breadcrumbs, popcorn, whatever grains I have on hand. Sometimes I make them a special treat of boiled chicken eggs or pasta bowties or sometimes, if I have extra coin, some minced seafood mash or worms from the fish market. They love that.

I scatter today's mix on the pavement before me and toss a few handfuls into the grass beyond. That's the call to arms, that food. All at once they surround me with their fluttering and squawking and bickering. Black and shimmering in the evening light—what beauties! Here and there a pigeon joins in, or a mourning dove (though those're really the same bird, ain't they?), or some songbirds. I don't mind. There's plenty.

"Here now, Jerrald," I call to one of my favorites. "Share with your brother!" Those two are always fighting. For all that Jerrald's getting up in age, he's been a bully for most of his seventeen years. Not likely he'll stop now, is it?

And look! There's Fiona! Sure, she's a crow. I know, I know she's white. Odd, ain't she? Fiona don't come every day, but I always bring her a special treat, just in case. I dig in my pocket and pull out a sliced apple wrapped in plastic.

"Come, Fiona!" I hold out a chunk and the nearer birds croak and flap, but I push 'em back. "No, eat your own food." I offer it again and Fiona comes first to the arm of the bench, then hops up to the back and inches closer until she can snatch the fruit from my hand. She tickles me the way she works up her courage, and I chortle a bit before I reach for another slice. She might be good for one more before she joins the rest of 'em on the ground.

I love these outings! Oh, I don't get around much anymore, except to go to the grocers or the fish market, but twice a day I come to the Common and sit across from the Great Elm marker. What would my babies do without me? I've watched some of 'em grow from fledglings into mated adults with fledglings of their own—not just Jerrald and Fiona, but Ralph and Bitsy and Bob and Sarah and Farley and all the rest. They're my family. Some of 'em will meet me at the Tremont stop and follow me past the plaza and the visitor center, cackling all the way to my bench. A few even visit me at home, a couple miles away, down to the Symphony. Can't feed them there, though. My windows open, and I can talk to 'em in the trees outside, but the only time I tried to take the screens off the windows, it busted the frames something awful. I almost got evicted. I ain't tried since.

In summer when the trees are full like they are now, I can almost forget my babies and I are surrounded by city. Almost. If I don't look up too often. Can't see the other monuments or even the bandstand from here. There's always people, though. Even this close to suppertime a few walk by, going around our big gathering. One toddler squeals with delight. The adults nod or speak. Most think I'm "that crazy bird lady." I don't mind. They're soon around the corner and out of my life, and their opinions matter less than a whit. You learn to think that way when you get old. Might have taken me longer than most, but at seventy years I finally figured it out. My life got easier after that.

Like those boys coming there. They'll be ones who think I'm crazy. I grunt to myself and throw out another handful of seed. "Eat up, sweetings! It's almost bedtime." It *is* later than I thought. Getting dark already. The kiddie park is quiet and frogs are singing over to the pond. Streetlamps are on down the way, and lights in surrounding buildings twinkle like stars against the sky. Must have lost track of time. That happens sometimes, these days. I toss more mix onto the grass and pick up my sack to head home for the night.

Loud clucking and flapping gets my attention and I look up. The boys have not gone 'round the birds. They're plowing *through*, kicking my babies as they go.

"Here now!" I yell. "Stop that! They ain't hurting you!"

"Shut up, old biddy," snaps the littlest one. I say little, but he's taller than me. What is he, fifteen?

The other two laugh.

My birds tilt their heads to watch this new show.

The biggest boy jerks his chin toward me. "What's in the bag, gramma?"

"Nothing," I huff. Dang pushy youngsters ain't gonna bully me. I roll down the top and cram the sack under my coat. "And if I was your gramma, you'd have better manners."

I fumble to my feet. The middle boy pushes me back down onto the bench. *Keep your mouth shut, Ana,* I tell myself. But I never listen, do I?

"Don't touch me, you little snot. If I had my cane, I'd show you what for!"

The big one's face curls into what might pass for a smile if you were half-blind. "Well, I guess we're lucky you don't have it, ain't we?" He steps closer. Too close. "Give us the sack and your wallet, and we'll leave you alone."

The sun's down now, and still my birds sit watching. Well now, that's odd, ain't it? Any other day, they'd be off before dark. I glance around. Not another human soul in sight. Huh. Guess I'll have to teach these boys a lesson my own self.

"I ain't giving you squat." I push toward the edge of the bench again and the big boy doesn't move. "Get out of my way."

He just stands there. I shove him aside and get to my feet. The other boys laugh. I don't care about that, but I do need to move on. This little encounter ain't setting my gut to ease. I totter off toward the bus, but ain't three steps away before they surround me again. One pushes my shoulder.

"Gimme the bag, gramma."

"No. Get away from me."

Another tries to snatch it out of my arms. I slap his hand away.

Now they're not laughing. Neither am I when they land the first punch.

My balance ain't what it used to be and I fall back, dropping the sack to cushion my head with both arms. I hear a snap when I land. I hear another when they kick me the first time. I curl into a ball best I can, cover my face and belly, but I don't remember much after that except pain and the taste of blood in my mouth and the screaming and flapping of my birds.

I wake in Mass General. Been here before, so the nurses know me. I'm not a regular or anything, but at my age sometimes a person needs a doctor. You understand. It's the little redhead's face I see first, all green eyes and freckles. I can never remember her name.

"Ana!" she sighs. "You're awake! Thank goodness..." She touches a button beside my bed.

I lick my lips, and she brings a straw to my mouth. I suck at the cool water. Best thing I've tasted in years. I try to speak, but all that comes out is a squawk. Sounds like Jerrald. I try again.

"How long?"

Red smiles. "You've been with us almost two days."

I try to raise my head, but she puts a firm hand on my shoulder. "Not yet. Take your time."

Two days ain't long enough? I want to ask, but I *am* a little fuzzy. For once I listen to my better judgment and stay quiet. The doc comes, takes my pulse, checks my IV, looks into my eyes with that little light they always carry. Listens to my chest. According to him, I'm lucky to be alive. Concussion, fractured arm, cracked ribs, bruised kidney, blah blah blah. I sigh. I kinda figured about the arm. Cast gave it away.

"Did I at least give as good as I got?"

He flashes Red a funny look before he smiles. "Let's just worry about you for now."

"How long before I can go home?"

"We'll see. You're mending well for your age, but it'll be at least a month before you'll be up and around on your own. Is there anyone at home to help you?"

I snort. *Sure. Got a whole staff.* "No."

"Then let's wait and see how it goes. Try to be patient. I'll see you later when I make my rounds."

When he's gone, Red fluffs my pillows and adjusts my blanket.

"There. Better?"

I nod. "Thanks."

"Anything else I can bring you?"

"How about some eggrolls?"

"Dinner's not for a few hours, but I'll see what I can find."

While she's gone, I look around. Like I said, I been here before, but not for long and never in a room with a window. The view ain't great, just a gravelly rooftop and the back side of the hospice wing across the way, but sunlight tells me it's after noon. Best of all, one of my birds sits outside on the ledge.

Jerrald.

Oh, the sight of him does my old heart good! I push the blankets away and sit up. Takes a bit of work, but I manage to get my legs over the side. Before I can slide down to my feet, Red comes running back.

"Ana! What on Earth are you doing? Honey, you're gonna hurt yourself! You can't be up and around yet!"

She don't know me very well.

I watch her set down my snack—which actually decides it, once my mouth gets to watering like that—and push myself back into position. She pulls the blankets over me, fussing the whole time. I listen with half an ear, and nod to pacify her. By the time Red leaves and I've eaten my rice, I'm sleepy again. I wake at the smell of dinner. Outside the window, the light's almost done and Jerrald's gone back to his roost. It ain't safe for a lone crow at night.

Or an old woman, either, apparently.

I think about those boys who put me here. Makes me mad, that. A month. I ain't got much, but my plants'll be dead by then. At least my rent payment is automatic. I twist best I can in the bed and reach around to open the top drawer in my nightstand. My keys. My lucky black feather. My little change purse. I pluck that out and open it. Empty. It wasn't just a sack of seed those boys were after.

I lean back against the bed and nod off despite the noisy hallway and the whining neighbors and the non-stop announcements over the P.A. Red wakes me a little later.

"Ana, the police are here. Feel like talking to them?"

"Sure." I straighten my hospital gown and push up taller in the bed. Red ushers them in and stays beside me the whole time.

"Ms. Ana Wilton?"

They already know that or they wouldn't be here. "Yes."

"Can you tell us what happened to you?"

I tell them about the birds, the boys, the sack, the punch, all the rest until everything went black.

"What did these boys look like?"

I try to remember their faces, but it's a blur. I describe them best I'm able. It ain't much. "I know I hit at least one of them little hooligans. I don't mean to hurt nobody, but they ought not be picking on old ladies in the park."

The officers open their mouths, but Red chases them out. I go back to sleep.

My eyes open to see the window. Jerrald is there with Farley. Noises from the hall sound like the breakfast cart's making its rounds. I glance around. Red will be off shift now.

I sit up, push the blankets back and grunt my legs over the side. Oh, I remember Red's words. Most of 'em anyway. So, I'm careful when I stand up. Legs are a little shaky and my side aches, but I use the IV pole like a walker and totter to the window before anyone stops me. I tap the glass. Jerrald blinks. Farley squawks. I wish I could hear him, but that'll come later when I'm back in the park. In a flutter of feathers, Farley's off and flying. Jerrald taps the glass with his bill and I chuckle.

"Oh yeah," I tell him. "Ain't no boys can put me down for long."

"Ana, you shouldn't be out of bed."

I turn to find Candace (not Candy...she hates Candy...that's why I remember her name) pushing an empty wheelchair. She grins, and I sit while she holds it still.

"Thanks."

"You're welcome." She comes around to squat in front of me, in front of Jerrald. "Friend of yours?"

"Yeah," I say. "We go back a ways."

"I've seen you. In the park. Feeding the crows."

How do you answer something like that? I look at her.

"Don't you worry they'll hurt you?"

"Hurt me? My babies?" I blow a raspberry. "Not a whit."

"How long have you been doing it?"

"Oh," I sigh, "prolly longer than you been alive."

She laughs. "Fair enough. How do you feel?"

"Better. Can I go home today?"

Candace's lips pucker like she's actually considering my question. "Hmm. I doubt it. But Doctor Riley's on duty now. You can ask her when she makes her rounds."

"Then can I have some peanuts?"

She agrees and leaves me by the window with my solemn promise to ask for help before getting up. Then breakfast comes and I have to convince the intern to let me eat where I sit. Bitsy has taken Jerrald's place, and I talk to her through the glass. The doc sweeps through and helps me back into bed. I shove the peanuts into a bottom drawer in my nightstand. Sleep takes me away for a few hours, and when I wake, Ralph is on the ledge. Lunch and dinner and doctors and nurses and more peanuts and naps, but at least with the chair I can get close to my sentinels. They keep a closer watch than any of the staff.

Days pass. Almost a week before they transfer me to a rehab place that specializes in old people and sports medicine, like I'm some sort of geriatric athlete. I have to make a fuss to get more peanuts and a window, but at least my sweetings find me and take turns on the ledge while my strength improves. In two more weeks, I'm walking not just to the window, but up and down the hall. The only thing better than my first real shower—with my arm in a plastic bag—is when they take off my cast and doc tells me tomorrow is The Big Day.

I'm going home.

Farley's at the window. I tell him I'll be back in the Commons tomorrow, and he taps the glass. I know he knows. He'll spread the word.

That night, I can hardly sleep.

Next morning, my babies are absent from the ledge. I eat breakfast, get dressed and stuff my hoard of peanuts into every pocket of my coat, even a few in my bra. I walk beside the nurse with the empty wheel-chair—no way they're pushing me another inch in that thing, I don't care one whit for their rules—to the front exit to catch my bus. I walk out into the fresh air, fresh as it ever gets in the city, and take a deep breath. Around the entry and down the walkway, every lamppost, every branch on every tree is filled with crows. Jerrald. Fiona. Farley. Ralph and Bitsy and all the others, even a few I don't recognize.

I make it to the bus stop, surrounded by my family, and wait. The bus comes and I get on. Sarah flies just ahead of my window for five blocks before she disappears. I can hardly wait to sit on my bench. The peanuts are mashing my breasts. It's uncomfortable.

I get off at Tremont, a mite sooner than Symphony, but it don't matter what those docs say. I'm seeing my babies before I go home. Caws herald my return. Sentinels follow, my babies leapfrogging past one another to keep me under guard like chaperones or presidential security. I chuckle, do a little dance in the plaza. I've missed this place. I've missed my sweetings! Peanuts are poor fare to offer them for such good company, but it's all I have.

At least for today.

I make it to my bench, tireder than I want to admit. I settle with a sigh into my spot and begin pulling out peanut packets. Before me, a sea of black—with one white spot—spreads across the pavement and onto the grass, a squawking, fluttering, flapping, noisy mass of love. I open the first packet and throw a handful into the crowd.

"You should be careful," a voice says, and I jump. I didn't see her come up. "...feeding those birds."

I squint at her proper business suit and made-up face. How can she walk in those shoes? "Thank you, but I'll be fine."

She frowns. "They can be dangerous, you know."

"Crows?" I ask, peering at her. I shake my head. "I doubt that."

The woman shrugs. "Tell that to the boys they attacked a while back. Landed all three of them in hospital. Two died."

My hand falters. "Boys?"

"It was in the news. Didn't you hear?"

"I don't watch tv." I toss the peanuts. "When did this happen?"

The woman blows out a long breath, her eyes rolling toward the sky. "Oh, maybe three or four weeks ago?"

I look up into her face. "Here? In the city?"

"Yep. Right in this very spot. They had the whole area taped off for almost a week." She glances at her watch. "Anyway, you be careful."

I nod and watch her walk away. My babies sit quiet, a rare thing, and I turn my attention back to them. Every one watches me, head cocked, eyes bright, feathers gleaming.

"Three boys, you say? Huh. Now ain't that odd."

I toss another handful of nuts and open the next packet.

CALL TO ACTION

Did you like this book? Don't forget to leave a rating or, better yet, a review! Tell a friend about Drema's works, and where to find them!

<u>Sign up for Drema's newsletter!</u>

You'll get reviews, occasional sneak peaks at upcoming stories, project updates, news on Drema's appearances, garden pictures, and cat news. You'll also be the first to receive announcements about upcoming book releases, cover reveals, special promotions, and other juicy tidbits from Niveym Arts.

Follow Drema on Facebook and BlueSky (links below), or subscribe to her blog for adventures in indie publishing, personal news and adventures, and other random posts.

Facebook: facebook.com/NiveymArtsLLC
Bluesky: dremadeoraich.bsky.social
Blog: http://www.dremadeoraich.com

ACKNOWLEDGMENTS

Many thanks to past and present members of the Science Fiction and Fantasy Writers of Hampton Roads who contributed in some way to the spit, polish, and shine of these stories over the years.

Thanks to the editors and staff of the magazines who saw and loved these stories when they were submitted, and who helped me bring them to the eyes of their readers:

All Worlds Wayfarer, https://www.allworldswayfarer.com/

Aphotic Realm Magazine. Alas, this journal now appears to be defunct.

Assymetry Journal of Speculative Fiction. Alas, this journal now appears to be defunct.

Daikaijuzine Magazine, https://www.daikaijuzine.org/

Electric Spec Magazine, https://www.electricspec.com/

Entropy. Alas, this online zine is now closed.

Mithila Review, https://mithilareview.com/

Silver Blade Magazine. This journal will always hold a special place in my heart, as they were the first magazine to ever publish one of my stories—"Last Call." Alas, this journal now appears to be on hiatus and/or defunct.

Thanks to Ollie and the team at 100 Covers for listening to my random ramblings about cover ideas and designing one that's perfect for this book.

And most of all, thanks to the B Man, my ongoing source of encouragement and support, and my number one fan. I love you, Silly Man.

ABOUT THE AUTHOR

Drema Deòraich is the author of award-winning speculative fiction that sometimes asks big questions. Her short works included herein have been published in numerous online journals, as well as a few semi-professional zines.

Her medical sci-fi/climate fiction novel *Entheóphage* explores the question, "What would it take to make us stop destroying our ecosystems?" "Phagey" (as it is affectionately known by its fans) has become a subject of book club discussions in many places.

Her science fantasy trilogy, *The Founder's Seed* (*Fallen, Book 1; Broken, Book 2;* and *Driven, Book 3*) explores what it means to be a misfit, the price you pay for stepping up when no one else can or will, and the life-altering journey to finding one's niche.

The follow-up trilogy, *Nexus,* is in the works, and tackles issues of human (and unammi) trafficking, what it means to be homeless, and the shadowy boundaries between law-abiding citizens and those outside the law who work for the common good.

Two of her novelettes, *Deer in Headlights* and *Jane Doe #7,* are both currently available in ebook format through Kindle Unlimited.

Other stories, like *Cleanup Crew,* are in the works. Stay tuned.

Drema currently lives in Southeast Virginia with her husband, his two cats, and all her other characters. When time and mosquitoes permit, Drema works on transforming the their yard into more welcoming habitat for small wildlife. She also occasionally blogs about writing, ideas from Life that inspire her, environmental issues, ways to live more sustainably, and whatever else captures her fancy. Follow her writing posts at http://www.dremadeoraich.com and her environmental posts at http://www.niveymarts.com.